SHE

A gripping serial killer detective thriller

PETE BRASSETT

THE
BOOK
FOLKS

First published by The Book Folks

London, 2017

© Pete Brassett

ISBN 978-1-5208-3026-1

www.thebookfolks.com

Present: Tense. Past: Imperfect.

CHAPTER 1

"SO. HOW DID YOU MEET?"

Fluke. Pure chance. I was at Harry's place, his bar on Rivington Street. Running a glorified pub wasn't something he'd planned or dreamed about, it wasn't something he'd hankered after, it just sort of happened.

My fault, I think. You see, if there was anything Harry was short of, it was drive. Ambition. If there was anything he had a surplus of, it was his inherent ineptitude at concentrating on anything remotely concerned with making a living. Simply because he didn't have to. Not that he was dim. Quite the opposite. He was smart, astoundingly so. One of those clever types with a mind like an Intel chip who understood string theory and the power of a neutrino but would fall to pieces if someone asked him to turn on the oven.

Some people said he was lazy. Just another lazy, rich kid with a silver spoon wedged firmly in his mouth. They blamed his parents for being too soft. Maybe they had a point but I didn't see it like that. From where I was standing, they were simply supporting him, and let's face it, they could afford to. Money to them was like confetti at a wedding. They're the kind of people who used £50 notes to light the barbecue, bought a new car when the old one ran out of petrol and thought nothing of doting on their only child until he found his way in the world. Found his 'niche'. I don't think 'publican' was the 'niche' they had in mind but they weren't disappointed, they ran with it. It got him out of a hole.

Harry, you see, despite his foibles, was just an average guy, albeit a privileged one, an average guy beset by boredom, cursed by wealth and addicted to booze. He was an alcoholic. He didn't drink to suppress his emotions or because he was hiding some sordid secret from his past. He drank simply because he was bored. That's what he told me, anyway. Funny, I couldn't help but think there must be another reason, I mean, you don't become an alcoholic just because you're bored. Or do you? Either way, I didn't pry; all I knew was, it was killing him. I'd badgered him for months to cut back and slow down before his body gave his liver an eviction notice but whatever I said fell on deaf ears. I grew frustrated. I think he must've been a Taurean because he was as stubborn as hell. So stubborn I resorted to going behind his back. I spoke to his parents. I told them they were killing him with kindness and, much as it may hurt, they had to be hard with him. Tough love. They agreed reluctantly whilst knocking back the Chablis and said they'd speak with him. They couldn't turf him out – for someone in his condition, that would've sealed his fate – so they threatened to withhold his allowance unless he got a grip and sorted himself out. He did. Well, he tried. And he failed. He joined AA. Lasted one meeting. Almost. He got as far as 'My name is Harry' before launching a tirade of abuse at the other members of the group, accusing them all of being spineless, work-shy misfits with uneducated palates who wouldn't know a decent Brouilly if it leapt up and bit them in the face. As a parting shot, he suggested they all sign up to a wine tasting course and do something useful with their lives before levanting for a night of passion with Laurent Perrier.

I could see him ageing before my eyes, withering like a dehydrated hydrangea, so I decided to give it one last try. I promised myself that if he didn't listen, if he didn't give up, then it was out of my hands and I could do no more than pen a witty eulogy and raise a glass to his passing. It was about a week later. We were at his parents' house. In his quest to find someone he could hold on to at night and wake up with in the morning, he'd invited a couple of twenty-something socialites to dinner in the vain hope that one of them would find the charms of a deluded dipsomaniac thoroughly irresistible. Neither did. The only thing they were interested in was the chateaubriand. Were it not for etiquette, they'd have licked their plates. They didn't hang around after that, didn't even wait for dessert. Mummy was unwell. Apparently.

We were on the terrace, he lamenting the loss of a potential partner who, incidentally, had all the charm of a spoiled brat and laughed like a horse while I, well, I think I was willing the sun to set so the evening would draw to a close. I watched as he uncorked a third bottle and decided to broach the subject before he slipped into oblivion. He wasn't one for reading, mainly because he couldn't focus on a page, so I'd already decided self-help books were not an option. Instead, I suggested he confront his demons, face them head on. I said, 'Look, if you have a fear of heights, you should walk a tightrope. If you have a fear of water, you should go swimming. Thing is, you don't fear the booze, but you should. Give it your best shot. See who comes out on top.'

I didn't expect him to take me seriously, at best I thought he'd go on a bender, get the mother of all hangovers, then start over again. He didn't. The following day he announced he was opening a bar and if he didn't drink it dry, he'd be cured. His mother and father, excited at the prospect of their son entering the world of brasseries and Michelin stars, tossed him a bundle of notes and the use of a cheque book. Two months later, the bar was open and I was worried. I needn't have been. By the end of the first week he'd consumed so much alcohol, he'd grown tired of the taste. By the end of the second week he'd spent so much time changing barrels and cleaning out slop trays, he'd grown sick of the smell. And by week three, the very thought of drinking it turned his stomach. And that, as they say, was that. Five years he'd been clean. No Michelin stars but then again, I don't think they award them for cheese toasties.

I digress. How did we meet? Well, like I say, I'd dropped by to see Harry. No particular reason, other than to say hello. Make sure he was still securely fastened to that wagon, after all, we were friends. Not the kind who socialised together, we didn't 'hang out' but we had each other's backs. There was a kind of distance between us, which actually kept us close, if you know what I mean. We never indulged in idle banter. If one of us spoke, the other listened.

Anyway, he was busy behind the bar, scowling at customers, slicing limes and doing his best to be as unwelcoming as possible. I sat patiently with an ice-cold Guinness and waited for the early evening rush to recede. That's when I noticed her. She was so… so incongruous. She had class. A short, summer dress, a pair of Cons and no make-up in a sea of stilettos, Tandoori tans and enough lip-gloss to coat the QEII. She sat with her back straight while her friends, three of them, slouched and giggled. She sipped sparkling water while they glugged Pinot. She caught my eye, smiled coyly and slowly looked away. I waited a while, not too long, then glanced back. She was gone. It's funny, I remember the feeling I got when I saw she wasn't there. It was a strange feeling of vague disappointment. I'd never experienced that before. I heard a woman howl, more of a cackle really, and turned to see the tail end of her group spilling on to the street. Harry whistled, like a shepherd calling his collie, and placed a pint on the bar. One of the perks of knowing the owner. I fetched my drink and returned to find my seat occupied. By her. She smiled. I'll never forget that smile. It was far too wicked for a face so innocent. I asked, jokingly, if she was stalking me. She smiled that smile again and said she'd wanted to meet me, that I looked 'intriguing'. 'Dirty'. And she didn't mean unwashed. She declined the offer of a sparkling water with imported Italian bubbles and opted for a Bloody Mary instead. The works. Everything except the celery. She hated celery. Apparently. An hour passed, it may have been two. I wasn't keeping track.

Lord knows what we talked about but the time flew by. It wasn't late, about eight o'clock I think, but it was time to leave. She concurred and rather generously announced that I was entitled to walk her as far as the tube station. I did. Then the ticket hall, then the platform and then onto the carriage. We didn't speak for twenty minutes. It was too loud, too crowded – a mass of tangled, perspiring arms clinging to germ-riddled grab-rails as though their lives depended on it. When she alighted at my stop I was, shall we say, a little unnerved. I mean, what were the chances of her living near me? The odds must have been fantastical. I concluded she was either stalking me after all or was after a one-night stand. The latter seemed improbable, she simply didn't seem the type, so I offered to walk her home, just to be sure. I wanted to see her put a key in the door and disappear from view. She did. I was, strangely, relieved and felt a tad guilty for casting aspersions on her character. I went home and realised I didn't even know her name. Her address, yes, but not her name.

The following morning was the same as any other. The unavoidable, habitual routine designed to hasten my departure; 6am. I showered while the kettle boiled, slurped a cup of tea while I smoked a cigarette, then dressed in the same, old jeans. That's where the similarity ended. I opened the front door and there she was. Smiling. A tingle ran up my spine, half excitement, half fear. Maybe 'fear' is too strong a word but you know what I mean. There was something about her, something dangerous. I asked if she'd camped out all night or followed me home. She laughed. No, she'd simply asked Harry for my address. Another tingle. She wasn't heading for the tube; she didn't work in town. The previous night had been nothing more than a social sojourn into the smoke to catch up with friends she knew she'd probably never see again. She worked in the archive department at the library on Vestry Road. I could see why. She was ordered, methodical. Sorting, numbering, listing, logging, filing. It suited her. I didn't ask why she was hovering by the gate, and that's odd. You'd have thought that that would have been the first thing on my mind – 'what are you doing here? what do you want?' – but no, the words never made it past my lips. She left, smirking, and walked towards the bus stop while I headed in the opposite direction.

I called Harry. I asked him if he remembered the girl in the bar, the girl in the yellow dress and Converse trainers. I asked him if he knew her. He did. I couldn't believe it. Must be that '6 degrees of separation' thing. Not only that, they had a history, too. An intimate history. The words 'dark' and 'horse' sprang to mind. For some reason I wasn't shocked, even though they were an unlikely pairing: she, petite and delicate; he, six feet four and built like a scrumhalf. He told me, briefly, that they'd met soon after he'd opened the bar. Turns out she'd helped him through the Battle of the Bottle, got him straight, kept him on an even keel. Said she reminded him of his ex, a skinnier version, shorter hair and, most importantly, not as bossy. Familiarity. I think that's why he kept her close. It made him feel comfortable. Couple of years they were together but not as, what you might call, a conventional couple. Seems they never lived together, they never took a holiday together and neither celebrated Christmas or birthdays in the company of the other but, for a time, they must have

needed each other. He asked if I was going to see her
again. I said I had a feeling that wasn't going to be for me
to decide.

CHAPTER 2

SPRATT HALL ROAD, WANSTEAD. 6:55am

From his office on the third floor, D.I. Munro was afforded a view normally reserved for roofers and steeplejacks. He sipped his tea – white, three sugars – and watched from the open window as a lone female – tall, mid-twenties – played enthusiastically with her retriever amongst the chestnuts and the sycamores on the green below. She stopped abruptly – perturbed by something untoward, something unexpected – spun on her heels and called for the dog to follow. Munro's eyes darted to the left, tracking her intended route, and settled on a drunk dangling precariously from a bench, the ground beneath him littered with empty beer cans. It was a recent phenomenon, not as bad as the jakeys and the junkies that lay strewn about the streets of Dumfries, but it was unacceptable, nonetheless. He buzzed the Desk Sergeant, advised him of the inebriate sleeping al-fresco across the way, and suggested he introduce him to a cell before the school run commenced.

He checked his diary. One entry. One more than the previous day, and the day before that. 11:45am. Snaresbrook Crown Court. Sentencing. Burglary. He'd be back in time for lunch. At the foot of the page he'd scribbled: 'D.S. West'. Finally, he thought, he'd have someone to talk to.

Disillusioned with the raft of cutbacks at 'The Mount', and still smarting from the untimely passing of his beloved Jean, Munro had postponed his retirement and moved south to escape the suffocating solitude of his memory-laden Larchfield home. With the Met employing the same cost-cutting techniques as his hometown, it wasn't the distraction he'd hoped for. He finished his tea, sighed and wondered, momentarily, if he should have surrendered his badge when he had the chance. Compared to life on the streets of Dumfy, where his investigative prowess was tested to the limit on a daily basis, his role down south was as taxing, and as interesting, as life in a retirement home.

The shouts from the street, though unintelligible, were undeniably threatening; the dialect, eastern European. Polish, perhaps. Or Romanian. It was impossible to tell. He watched, despondently, as two of his constables steered their staggering quarry back to the station, knowing full well he'd be back on the streets by nightfall.

The phone buzzed. Internal. Front desk confirmed the arrival of their guest and advised him that a certain Detective Sergeant West was on the way up.

Munro checked his tie in the small, framed mirror hanging from the bookcase, patted down what was left of his thinning, grey hair and wiped an unwelcome scuffmark from the toe of his polished, leather walking boots. He stood, back to the window, hands clasped behind his back and ensured his expression was suitably stern. A short, sharp rap rattled the door.

'Hello, lassie,' he said, peering over her shoulder. 'What can I do for you?'

'Detective Inspector Munro? James Munro?'

'Aye, that's right. I don't mean to be rude, but I'm expecting someone the noo.'

'D.S. West, sir.'

'That's right, how did you know? Is he with you?'

'I am Detective Sergeant West, sir.'

'You?' said Munro, mildly surprised. 'I… I was…'

'You were expecting a man. Sorry to disappoint you.'

'No, no, I'm not disappointed, just a wee bit…'

'Surprised.'

'Aye. That's the word. Surprised.'

'And you don't like surprises?'

'I do not.'

Munro looked on as D.S. West, smirking slyly to herself, commandeered the empty desk and made herself at home. He regarded her approvingly, attired as she was in a green hiking jacket, black jeans and sturdy boots, and couldn't help but think she would have looked more at home clambering up The Devil's Beef Tub or sheltering in a bothy.

'Well, once you've unpacked,' he said, testing her, 'perhaps you'd like to make some tea. Kettle's just there.'

D.S. West did not, as expected, rise to the bait.

'Sorry, Braveheart,' she said, smiling broadly, with scant regard for his rank. 'I don't make tea for anyone, unless they're in my house.'

Munro allowed himself the smallest of smiles, happy at the arrival of his foil.

'Humility is an admirable trait,' he said. 'Often lacking in the younger generation, but I'm not too proud to put the kettle on myself. What'll you have?'

She reached into her bag and tossed him a box.

'One of these, please.'

'Chamomile?' said Munro.

'Yes, it's herbal. What they call an infusion.'

'Is that so? Well, well, well.'

They sat quietly at their respective desks, each cradling their cup, each watching the other like a couple of steely-eyed poker players, waiting to see who would crack first. Munro correctly assumed his partner to be in her late twenties. Her tousled brown hair was pinned precariously atop her head. Her complexion was fresh and attractively weathered. Her eyes, hazel. As were Jean's. Judging by her accent, she wasn't a Londoner. Too eloquent. More home counties. Berkshire, he imagined, or Surrey. Somewhere spacious enough for her ponies. He drained his cup.

'Well now, Sergeant,' he said, opting to break the silence. 'It wouldn't do to call you Westie for the foreseeable. Folk will think I'm calling a hound. So, tell me, do you have a first name?'

* * *

Unlike certain officers she'd worked with in the past, officers who hid behind a stereotyped façade laden with bravado and expletives, there was something charming about Munro. The way he carried himself, his actions, slow but deliberate; his Celtic brogue, soft and lilting. She locked eyes with his, disarmingly bright and blue, and caught a glimpse of the man beneath. Someone as hard as nails.

'Charlotte,' she said, almost blushing.

'Charlotte! Why, that's an elegant name,' said Munro, rising from his desk. 'Which do you prefer, Charlotte, is it Lottie? Or Lola, perhaps…'

'I prefer Charlotte, sir.'

'Good. Charlie it is, then,'

She shook her head and smiled.

'If you don't mind me saying so, Charlie, you look a wee bit… young, to be a Sergeant. A Detective Sergeant, at that.'

'I'll take that as a compliment,' said West, leaning back and grinning.

'Please do.'

'I'm old enough, if that's what you're thinking.'

'Oh, I'm not after your age,' said Munro, 'it would be rude of me to ask. You've worked your way up, then? Paid your dues, as they say?'

'Of course! I've…'

11

'Good. Call me old-fashioned, but I'd hate to think you were one of those university types, you know, the graduates who join the force and leapfrog their way to promotion just because they have a degree or two instead of pounding the streets, doing it the hard way, as it were.'

From the pained expression on her face, it was obvious to Munro that, unless she was in dire need of root canal surgery, he'd hit a nerve.

'It takes brains as well as brawn,' she said, defensively. 'I've been out there with the best of them. I've felt a few collars, as they say.'

Munro returned to his desk, eased himself into his chair and, with his hands clasped beneath his chin, regarded her like a doctor assessing a patient. He smiled gently with a reassuring tilt of the head, aware that her confidence had tripped the line to arrogance.

'Let's not get off on the wrong foot, lassie. I'm not questioning your ability. I'm just curious, I like to get the measure of the folk I work with. That's all.'

West relaxed and finished her drink.

'That's alright, then,' she said, curtly. 'And just for the record, I've worked bloody hard to get where I am. I've earned the right to be here, you know.'

'I'm sure you have,' said Munro, smiling. 'So, how long have you been a D.S., Charlie?'

'Eighteen months, sir. Nearly.'

'Eighteen months? Why, you're an old hand at the job, lassie. And what have you bagged, so far? A few stolen cars, I expect. The odd burglary, perhaps; maybe even an armed robbery?'

'I should be so lucky,' said West, glibly. 'Mainly assaults and road rage. There was one hold-up, no shooters, though. Guildford isn't really the place for them.'

'Guilford? So you transferred? Life a wee bit dull in the suburbs?'

'You could say that,' said West. 'Thought things might be a little more interesting with the City.'

12

'And that's what you're after, is it, Charlie?' said Munro. 'Action?'

'Yes, sir. I'd like…'

'You'd like to feel your knees turn to jelly when you approach a rucksack someone's left on the concourse at, let's say, Liverpool Street station? Afraid it'll blow up in your face?'

'Well, not exactly, I mean…'

'You'd like to feel your bowels loosen when some bampot in Hatton Garden holds a pistol to your head, knowing he's not afraid to use it because to him, you are the scum of the earth?'

'I hadn't thought of it like…'

'Well, you'd better start thinking,' said Munro, fixing her with a steely gaze and lowering his voice, as if delivering a mournful lament, 'you've not even scratched the surface, lassie.'

'I don't follow,' said West, 'just because…'

'Have you never walked a railway track in search of a limb or two? An arm or a leg that's been severed from the body by an Intercity train? Have you not tried to scrape the remains off the track, scrape it because the voltage has fused the flesh to the line? Have you never had to knock the door and tell the parents that wee Jimmy's dead? And all because of a game of chicken?'

D.S. West sat, ashen-faced, at once abhorred and enthralled.

'Do you know what it's like to wander round a derelict scheme in the dead of night, wading through pools of vomit and discarded needles, trying to reach a junkie who's pumped his body full of fentanyl, looked into his heroin eyes and seen nothing but despair? Or perhaps you've not yet experienced the feeling of utter helplessness when a young lass dies in your arms, just because some ned thought it was clever to drive at eighty miles an hour the wrong way up a one-way street?'

West fidgeted nervously in her seat as Munro's voice dropped to barely more than a whisper.

'Have you ever hauled a body from the canal? An anaemic, bloated carcass, bobbing on the surface like some inflatable whale, full of putrid, toxic gas, and heaved your guts up because the pike and the roach and the eels have eaten his eyes and his lips? Have you not experienced the frustration of trying to convict some nutter who's skelped his wife so badly she's in the infirmary but says nothing for fear of retribution? Stays quiet, even though she's been battered black and blue from head to toe?'

D.S. West simply shook her head.

'Then I assume you've never had to wipe another man's blood from your face either. And I hope to God, you never will.'

West sat perfectly still, dumbfounded and shocked, as Munro slowly raised his arm and slammed the desk with the palm of his hand. She jumped.

'So, Charlie!' he said, smiling broadly. 'Let's lighten the mood a little, tell me now, why did City of London send you here? Surely, whatever you did can't have been that bad?'

West's shoulders slumped with relief, as if she'd just been given the all clear. Flustered, and slightly unnerved, she cleared her throat, took Munro's cup from his desk, and switched on the kettle.

'Pulled the short straw, sir,' she said nervously. 'I'm afraid no-one else wanted to work with Taggart.'

'Taggart?' said Munro.

'You've a reputation.'

'I'm flattered.'

'It's a missing person, sir.'

'James, please,' said Munro, 'we're not on ceremony, here.'

'I think I'll stick with "sir", if that's alright with you. I'd like to maintain a sense of professionalism, hierarchy; then we know where we stand.'

Munro raised one corner of his mouth, nauseated at the waffle.

'In that case, Charlie, we'll have a little less of your lip. So, you're after a missing person, you say?'

'That's right,' said West. 'Chap by the name of Harry, Harry Farnsworth-Brown.'

'How many names does a fellow need?' said Munro.

'He's not been seen for four days,' said West. 'Today's the fifth. Completely out of character. Apparently. Even missed Saturday night, which is the busiest night of the week.'

'I don't follow.'

'He runs a bar.'

'I see. And who reported him missing?' said Munro. 'A loved one? His next of kin, perhaps?'

'Neither. Seems he's single. Unattached.'

'Family?'

'Parents. That's it,' said West, handing him a cup of tea. 'Father's American, an investment banker, retired; mother's British, a solicitor, retired too. Both on holiday. They've got a place in Sicily.'

'And you've checked their house?' said Munro, grimacing as he sipped his tea. 'He's not making use of the facilities while they're away?'

'We spoke to the cleaner and the gardener, they've not seen him for weeks. Uniform went round yesterday. Nothing.'

'And he's not the impulsive type? Could he not have taken himself off somewhere? A wee holiday, perhaps?'

'Not according to the bar staff. He's not missed a day in five years.'

Munro stood, walked purposefully to the table and tipped three, generous spoons of sugar into his cup.

'Bar staff?' he said.

'Yes,' said West. 'They're the ones who reported him missing. The manager, actually.'

'I see. And they've tried calling him, obviously?'

15

'They have. No response. Landline rings out and his mobile goes to voicemail. Oh, and his emails are bouncing, which can only mean his mailbox is full.'

Munro turned his chair to the window, sat down and stared out across the green.

'Unopened mail,' he said quietly. 'Like six pints of milk on the doorstep. A sure sign that someone's gone away.'

'But that's not like him,' said West. 'They say he's not the type to just…'

'When I say "gone away", Charlie, I mean it as a euphemism.'

'Oh,' said West, suddenly feeling out of her depth.

'Tell me,' said Munro, 'where, exactly, is this bar? This den of iniquity?'

'Shoreditch. Rivington Street.'

'Shoreditch? Why, Charlie, that's your patch, not mine.'

'It is now,' said West. 'I mean, he lives here, sir. Wanstead. Victory Road.'

'Victory Road?' said Munro, rubbing his chin. 'Let me think. I imagine that'll be the old orphanage, then.'

'Orphanage? What would he be doing…'

'It's not an orphanage now, lassie. It's a beautiful building, two hundred years old, at least, full of apartments. Big, fancy, expensive ones. You'd have to be a millionaire to live there, of that I'm sure. It used to be the Merchant Seaman's Orphan Asylum. Then a hospital. It's a twenty-minute walk. If that.'

'Can we take a look?' asked West.

'Take a look?' said Munro, aghast at the request. 'Are you telling me no-one's been already?'

'Er, no. Not really, I mean, a couple of beat officers from Snaresbrook looked in last night but there was nobody home.'

'And that's it? No door-to-doors? You've not met the neighbours? Taken a wee look inside his flat?'

'Well, no,' said West, adopting the stance of a scolded child. 'Not yet. I thought…'

16

'You thought...?'

'Well, he could have gone out, you know, for dinner or something, or down the pub.'

'I doubt it, lassie,' said Munro, reaching for his coat. 'I doubt it. Right, I think it's time you started earning your salary, don't you? You've got the address, ring down and ask for Sergeant Cole, tell him we need a car to meet us there. You and I will walk. Oh, and tell him to bring the "big key", too, we may have to give the door a wee nudge, so to speak.'

CHAPTER 3

"HOW WELL DID YOU KNOW HER?"
Are you kidding? Better than anyone. Inside out, back to front, upside down. I knew everything about her. Which, in a way, is odd. I mean, tell me, how well do we know anyone? Let's face it, you can know someone for thirty years and yet not really know them at all. That's why it's odd. I only knew her a couple of months. Weeks, in fact. I suppose it all depends on who you're talking to really, and how open they are with you, after all, it's the personal stuff that matters, isn't it? It's the personal stuff that allows you under their skin.

On the outside, she was very self-assured, confident, got on with everyone – an extrovert, you might say – but underneath it all she was actually a very private person. Very demure. I remember asking Harry about her, after all, they had a history. Nothing too specific, just general stuff. I wanted to see what I was getting myself in to. The best he could manage, after a couple of years in a so-called relationship, was 'yeah, she's fun, likes The Happy Mondays'. He didn't know her at all. He didn't even know she had a degree. Whatever we had, whatever you choose to call it – a dalliance, an affair, a partnership – our 'liaison' was intense. So yes, I knew her pretty well.

She relished revealing facts about herself, about the past, her present, it was like she was testing me, gauging my reactions, seeing if I'd make the grade. There was no hesitation, no beating around the bush, no fear of causing offence; she'd just come right out and say stuff as though she knew it wouldn't go any further, as though she knew she could trust me, which she could, implicitly. Like a priest but without the confessional. And always with that smile. The smile that told me I was about to become privy to something personal, something 'naughty'. No, not 'naughty'. Dark. Something 'dark', something she'd never shared before. I listened, intently. I wasn't there to judge, nor to question, nor to express an opinion. If I had, it would have ruined things. My role was simply to listen, which meant she smiled a lot.

It started the day after we met. I was looking forward to getting home. I'd had enough. Apart from the gallery postponing the private view and wanting to increase their commission, I'd locked myself out of the studio and ripped my jacket climbing in through the second-floor window. It was about half-six, seven maybe, and all I could think of was an ice-cold beer. I was halfway down the street, glanced up towards my house and saw her standing by the gate. Another tingle. Part of me wanted to turn around and disappear before she saw me, another part wanted to sneak up behind her, slap her on the backside and give her a kiss on the cheek. I went with the second, but without the slapping or the kissing. Or the sneaking for that matter. Truth be known, I was glad to see her, she made me feel, I don't know, different, even though it was like... like knowing that if you put your hand in the fire, you were going to get burned. Trouble is, I wanted to shove both arms in. Anyway, I feigned surprise and invited her in for, well, I don't know what for, a drink I suppose. Coffee or a beer, or a glass of wine. It would've been rude not to. As it happens, she declined. The rebuttal took me by surprise, particularly as it was her waiting for me, but there wasn't time for my pride to reel with rejection, she suggested we go to hers instead. Safe ground, I suppose. I didn't have time to argue, nor to go indoors for that matter. She slipped her arm in mine and marched me down the street. I knew where she lived. Cowley Road.

The house was a beautiful little terraced cottage. Two-up, two-down. Christ knows how she afforded it, I mean, on a salary from the library? I can only assume the Royal Bank of Winnersh helped her out. Winnersh. Funny name, that. It's in Berkshire, I think. Anyway, that's where she lived, or rather, her parents. It's where she grew up. She took my coat, sat me down and handed me a can of Guinness. She'd obviously made a note of what I'd been drinking the night before. She poured herself a large vodka and tomato juice, put on a CD – Vivaldi, The Four Seasons – and sat cross-legged on the floor in front of me, her skirt hitched up around her thighs. She smiled and asked me if I knew what an aneurysm was. Just like that. I said I did. Why? 'That's what killed my father,' she said, 'two days before my thirteenth birthday'. One day, fit and healthy; the next, not. Just collapsed in a heap on the way home from work. Brain aneurysm. Found him dead in the car. I was dumbfounded. Didn't know what to say. I was expecting a conversation about, I don't know, films or her job, or how long she'd lived in the area or... or if I was single. Not death. Not the demise of her father. She drained her glass, said something like 'Christ, I hate classical music' and played a Johnny Cash CD instead. Incidentally, she'd never heard of the Happy Mondays. She told me that her father had loved classical music. Everything from Prokofiev and Elgar to Haydn and Bach. Doesn't take a genius to figure out why she hated it.

Her father was buried. Cremation, her mother opined, was for Hindus, not Christians, and being interred in a casket six feet under was undeniably more civilised than being barbecued like a rack of ribs in front of your nearest and dearest. She didn't agree and, much to her mother's annoyance, let it be known that she would rather be guest of honour at a pyre party than be consumed by a variety of subterranean arthropods until she was nothing more than compost.

In the absence of a paternal figure to guide and encourage her, there came, soon afterwards, a turning point in her life. She gave up the violin and the horse riding, the piano lessons and the netball, and became, in her own words, 'a bit of a tomboy', obsessed with the outdoors and, in particular, creepy-crawlies. Insects. She smiled. By her own admission, she enjoyed nothing more than collecting earthworms and spiders from the acreage they called a garden, taking them to her room and curtailing their invaluable contribution to the ecosystem by pulling their legs off or slicing them up like a stick of salami.

It was past midnight when we finally ate something and even then, in between spoonfuls of lamb madras and pilau rice, she kept talking. It was a long night, I couldn't keep up. I fell asleep on the sofa with her lying next to me, huddled up against my chest like a limp ragdoll.

After that, we met with alarming regularity. Every night, in fact. It became ritualistic, a habit. Whether she regarded it as some sort of therapy, I don't know, but she seemed to benefit from it. Then again, maybe it was all a game to her, maybe she had a motive, maybe it had been her intention to snare me all along. If it was, she succeeded. I was hooked.

It wasn't all serious talk, though. I mean, it's not as if we spent every single moment together raking over the past. We had fun, too. We enjoyed each other's company, we were comfortable together. Very comfortable. We danced like teenagers around the lounge, we sang along to Mike Scott, we played games, she sat for me while I sketched her and eventually – I guess it was on the cards anyway – we became 'intimate'. By the time we'd got to that stage, which didn't take long, I knew she wasn't deranged or unbalanced; confused perhaps, a little mixed-up, but ultimately, lonely.

As an only child, that sense of loneliness, or rather, of being alone, enveloped her within weeks of her father's death. Surrounded by adults who preferred not to talk about it and school friends who were too young to understand, she bottled everything up and embarked on a period of self-harm. I know, a classic case of attention-seeking, wouldn't you say? But even then, at that young age, she was clever about it. She avoided doing anything obvious, anything that would raise eyebrows or land her with a care order. She contrived every incident to look like an accident. Not one, single, pre-meditated episode involved a knife, or scissors, her hair, pills, tablets or blood. She broke her bones instead.

It started with the little finger on her right hand. She snapped it with the left. Out of curiosity, she said. It didn't hurt. She smiled. It was somehow pleasurable. It went on for years, over which period of time, as a result of jumping from trees, stumbling down river banks, cycling into walls and playing with the vice bolted to the workbench in her father's shed, she'd managed to successfully break six of her eight fingers, both wrists, her left leg, her collar bone and an ankle. She was young, she healed quickly. Her mother put her boisterous behaviour down to her exuberant nature and a surplus of sugar in her diet. It never occurred to her that the problem might be more deep-rooted than that. She stopped snapping her appendages in her late teens when she discovered something else, quite by chance. She'd been darning a jumper. Sitting on her bed, darning her favourite jumper, when she accidentally pricked herself with the needle. On the inside of her thigh. If it had been me, I would have probably sworn. Most people would've yelped. She did not. She grinned as she told me how aroused she became when she pushed the needle in again and again, using her forefinger to demonstrate the action.

Although it never disappeared completely, her penchant for sticking sharp objects into her leg waned when she started university. She couldn't say why. I'm guessing it was the distraction, though I find it hard to believe Staffordshire could have that effect. It was her enthusiasm for bugs and small, flying insects which dine on human flesh that had led her there, convinced that her future lay buried in the world of entomology. By the end of the first term, she'd realised she'd made a mistake. Insects were ridiculously small and impossible to dissect. She switched courses and moved to Nottingham where she studied biology and became somewhat skilled in the use of a scalpel, slicing open anything to hand – rats, frogs, rabbits, hearts, livers. Anyway, she went on to gain a first and graduated with honours. I asked her why she didn't take it further, you know, take up a career in medicine, or pharmacology, perhaps. Actually, pathology would have been more appropriate. She admitted that during her final year, that seemed like the logical thing to do but something unexpected occurred, something which put her off studying for good. The senior lecturer. He was about twenty years older than her, not bad looking by all accounts, married with a nice wife, a nice house and nice kids. He took her under his wing, coached her, encouraged her, preyed on her all too obvious vulnerability. It was only a matter of time. They had a fling, what she described as a 'five-night stand'. When she realised her mistake, that the relationship was foolish and destined to failure, she told him it was over. He, however, thought otherwise. He'd become infatuated, obsessed almost, and despite her protestations, took to following her around campus, even turning up unexpectedly on her doorstep late at night to deliver an ultimatum: either they continued seeing each other or he would make sure she failed her degree. She relented, and agreed to see him one last time. She didn't go into detail, didn't tell me exactly what happened, she just smiled and asked if I knew what it was like to be circumcised whilst 'in flagrante'. That's when the tables turned. In return for not telling his wife of the affair, nor the board of governors, she gained her degree and took great delight in reading her bank statement a few weeks later where the balance was shown to be in credit by a staggeringly large amount. Enough for a deposit on a quaint, terraced cottage, no doubt.

I think that's what made her so... so charismatic. That's what intrigued me about her. The fact that, on the outside, she was sugar and spice and all things nice, but on the inside, she was snips and snails and puppy dogs' tails with an appetite for, well, anything not quite normal. And for someone so small, she had one hell of an appetite.

She was a die-hard carnivore and there was nothing she liked more than devouring a decent steak the size of the plate, swimming in blood. Oh, apart from steak tartare, that is. She called it steak tartare, I called it raw mince with an egg on top. For some reason, she enjoyed eating it with her bare hands. It wasn't a dish we shared. Like me, she balked at the idea of consuming anything green, anything called 'cereal' or anything labelled 'healthy' or 'low fat'. She was, what those who were jealous of her petite physique called, 'lucky' – lucky to have a high metabolism. I told her it had nothing to do with metabolism, more the fact that her diet was almost exclusively protein, and for breakfast, that meant eggs. Poached. On toast. Eggs Benedict if we went out. Scrambled, on a Sunday. With bacon. Dry-cured. Streaky.

She didn't own a television. Four million channels from around the world and not a single thing worth watching, unless, as she said, you were as vacuous and banal as the meaningless tripe that appeared on the screen. She listened to music instead, mainly John Denver, Willie Nelson or Andy Williams, stuff with a gentle refrain, played on an old stereo system bought for her on her 21st birthday. At night, she listened to the radio. 'Book at Bedtime'. It sent her to sleep.

She enjoyed reading. I thought she may have liked Salinger or Heller. Salinger would have suited her. Instead, I underestimated her level of intelligence and realised her masochistic tendencies stretched to literature when I perused the shelves. They were lined with the kind of volumes often seen on the returns desk at Waterstones or used to hold doors open. Solzhenitsyn, Tolstoy, Borges, Cervantes, Chekhov, Homer, Dostoyevsky and Flaubert, scattered in between medical journals and books on biology, immortality and Buddhism. Buddhism? That explained the meditation. Every evening, for an hour. I never had her down as the religious type but then, as she delighted in telling me, Buddhism was not a religion for there was no God, no redemption and no heaven. Buddhism is a moral, philosophical and ethical way to live in the here and now in the hope of escaping the cycle of Samsara and attaining the ultimate state of Nirvana.

I wittily pointed out that she was still in the cycle of Samsara, proof of which was the birthmark, shaped like Denmark, on the small of her back. Nothing large or obtrusive, not that it troubled her. She said 'why should I be bothered about something I can't even see?'. Her back was her soft spot, the vulnerable area where she liked to realise those mild, masochistic tendencies which were, no doubt, a legacy of her youth. She enjoyed having her back scratched. Hard. And that was a revelation. I mean, not wholly unexpected, but for someone who looked so 'innocent', it was like finding out that Mary Poppins was into bondage. She'd lie there, face down, sweating and groaning while I clawed it to pieces. The more it bled, the more she groaned. Looked like she'd been lashed with a cat o'nine tails. She asked if I'd ever dripped hot wax on anyone before. That smile. A tingle. She kept the candles in the cutlery drawer.

CHAPTER 4

VICTORY ROAD, WANSTEAD. 8:47am
Apart from the colossal stained-glass windows and the terracotta brickwork, the most noticeable feature of the old orphanage, an imposing, Venetian-style building, was the clock tower.

'Are you sure this is it, sir?' said West as they strolled through the landscaped gardens, oblivious to the squad car parked by the communal entrance. 'I was told the address was Clock Court.'

Munro stopped in his tracks.

'Charlie,' he said. 'I know it's not a name that fires the imagination but, unfortunately, it was the best those clever wee marketing men could do when they hacked this magnificent building to pieces. Just look up there; look and tell me, what do you see?'

West, befuddled, ignored the morning sun bouncing off the glowing brickwork and regarded the building with an air of indifference.

'Well,' she said hesitantly. 'It looks like an old hospital, and a bit like a church, I suppose. Just an old building, really. It's alright. Bit old.'

Munro heaved a sigh and gazed up at the tower.

'A bit old? I despair. What we have here, Charlie, is a unique example of Gothic-influenced, eighteenth century architecture; two hundred years of history, magnificent enough to inspire poets and artists, and all those philistines could do was look no farther than that wee clock up there. Hence the name. Incidentally, it doesnae work.'

'Oh,' said West, unimpressed. 'Shall we? Second floor, flat C.'

Munro shook his head and glanced around the rows of parked cars.

'Hold on,' he said. 'Does he have a motor car?'

'Sorry?'

'This Farnsworth-Brown fellow, does he have a motor car? Could he have driven off somewhere?'

'I...'

'You've not checked, have you?'

West cursed under her breath, snatched a notebook from her jacket pocket and scribbled furiously on a blank page.

'I'll do it as soon as we...'

'That you will, Charlie. That you will.'

* * *

Two officers stepped from the car. One, a Police Community Support Officer, looked on as his superior, Sergeant Tommy Cole, wearing a helmet and body armour, retrieved the 'enforcer' from the boot. They climbed the hollow stairwell to the second floor in silence and hovered outside the apartment. Munro glanced down the corridor. Stud walls, a tired carpet and four anonymous-looking doors. He nodded. West knocked the door. No answer. She knocked again. They waited.

'Right, lad,' Munro said, addressing the Support Officer, 'try the other flats, see if anyone's seen or heard anything of our friend.' Stepping back, he winked at the other officer and grinned. 'Okay, Tommy,' he said, 'let's take a look inside.'

The door flew open with a single strike, taking the architraving and deadbolts with it. They stood, stock still, holding their breath, waiting, listening, for any signs of life.

'After you,' said Munro.

They filed in, Sergeant Cole first, followed by West. Munro gasped as he entered the apartment.

'Holy Mother of God,' he said, gazing skyward, 'will you look at the height of that ceiling. How on earth is one expected to clean up there? It's cavernous. Aye, that's the word. Truly cavernous.'

The sparse furnishings made the entire apartment appear even larger than its 1,500 square feet. The timber-clad, vaulted ceiling, two mezzanine levels and wrought iron staircases, held them in awe. Munro stood, speechless, bathed in a single shaft of sunlight that streamed, almost religiously, through a huge, arched window.

'You could fit ten of my house in here,' he said, turning slowly on his heels.

'Probably twenty of mine,' said West.

'I'm saying nothing,' said Cole.

The PCSO, an ex-traffic warden, ex-reservist and volunteer steward at his local football club, shattered the reverential stillness with his brash, Bermondsey brogue.

'Bloody Nora!' he said, pushing his cap to the back of his head. 'It's like the bleedin' Tardis.'

Munro, taken aback by the rambunctious intrusion, regarded him contemptuously.

'The Tardis? Perhaps you'd care to journey somewhere?' he said quietly. 'It can be arranged.'

'Sir.'

'Well, what did you find?'

'Not much luck, sir,' said the PCSO, straightening his cap. 'Flat A, no answer. Flat B was answered by a Lithuanian gentleman whose grasp of the English language, I have to say, left a lot to be desired.'

'I see,' said Munro, rapidly tiring of the Officer's monotonous delivery.

'Incidentally, if you don't mind, sir, I'm going to request that we pay him another visit. There's about eleven people living there, sure Immigration might have something to say about it.'

'As you will,' said Munro. 'And the other...'

'Just coming to that, sir. The other flat, flat D, directly opposite, was occupied by a very helpful chap. Scottish. From Glasgow, he says.'

'Glasgow, indeed?' said Munro, with a wry grin. 'Well, well, well, looks like the area's on the up, at last.'

'He said he last saw Mr Farnsworth-Brown about a week ago. They passed on the stairwell, exchanged pleasantries. That was it. Oh, said he was with a young lady, on their way out, they were.'

'Excellent,' said Munro. 'And do you not think it might be useful to have a description of this young lady?'

'Probably.'

'Well?' sighed Munro. 'What are you waiting for, man? Go get it. Right, Charlie, Tommy, down to work. Gloves please, ladies and gentlemen.'

West scurried up the stairs to the mezzanine level while Munro sauntered through to the small, almost afterthought of a bathroom. Arms folded, he leaned forward and scrutinised the tiles around the tub and the shower. Clean. Not even a watermark. A single toothbrush languished in a plastic beaker by the wash basin. Dry. He sniffed the air. The faintest of odours wafted up from a bale of towels piled high on a stool. Fabric conditioner. They had not been used. Next door was the kitchen. It too was so disproportionately small it was suitable only for those who despised cooking and lacked the inclination to wash dishes. The worktop was spotless. No cups. No plates. No pans. The fridge, empty. Not even a pint of milk. The kettle, half full. Cold. Mr Farnsworth-Brown, concluded Munro, was either on a diet or employed an impressively meticulous cleaner. He winced at the sound of West screeching from above.

'Sir!' she wailed. 'Got something!'

Munro swore under his breath.

'Leave it, lassie!' he yelled back. 'Don't even breathe on it, do you hear?'

He trudged up the spiral staircase and paused at the top to take in a bird's eye view of the apartment.

'Something wrong?' asked West, with a frown.

'Altitude sickness,' said Munro, glancing towards the bed. 'He's not slept here, either.'

'Sorry?'

'The bathroom's not been touched and the kitchen's bare, there's not even a stale Garibaldi in the cupboard. And his bed, it's all made up like they do in a hotel. The only thing that's missing is a wee mint on the pillow. So, what have you got?'

West pointed to a side table.

'Phone,' she said as Munro dropped to his knees and squinted at the handset, 'almost missed it, being white on white; it's what they call a smartphone, not like the old...'

'A smartphone?' said Munro. 'Is that so? And there was I thinking it was an iPhone, a 4s by the looks of it, you can tell by the size of the screen, you know. Now, come here and squat beside me, you might learn something.'

West, feeling suitably belittled for her patronising comment, knelt silently beside him.

'Now, Charlie,' he said, almost whispering, 'lower your head till you catch the light, take a good look and tell me what you see.'

West bit her lip as she pondered her response.

'Come on, lassie, we've not got all day.'

'I give up,' she said. 'There's nothing here. Nothing but the phone. And dust.'

Munro broke a satisfied smile.

'Hallelujah,' he said. 'Well done.'

'Really? Are you being sarcastic?' said West.

'Look at the phone, again,' said Munro. 'Look closely. What do you see?'

West hesitated.

'No dust,' she said with a smug grin.

'We'll make a detective of you, yet,' said Munro. 'So, what does that tell us?'

'That the phone hasn't lain here for a week? That… that it was placed here recently?'

'Exactly. And very carefully at that.'

Munro pulled a small flashlight from his pocket.

'Are you alright, sir?' said West. 'Do you want the lights on? Glasses?'

Shaking his head, Munro directed the pale blue beam at the phone.

'It's an FLS, lassie. A Forensic Light Source. Did they not teach you anything? The phone's been cleaned, not even a smudge of a print. It's spotless. Whoever placed it here, knew exactly what they were doing.' He stood and stretched his back. 'We need to know if anyone else has a key to this place, see what you can find out. I want forensics down here quick as you like, doors, floor, the lot; then get the phone away for analysis, see what you can get off it.'

'Sir.'

Sergeant Cole was waiting by the door.

'Been all over, guv, nothing obvious; place has been cleaned by the looks of it. If he was here, he's either been abducted by aliens or he's spontaneously combusted.'

Munro grinned.

'Don't talk daft, Tommy, there's no scorch marks. Right, I'm away, I'm due in court in twenty minutes. I'll see you back at the office. Just in time for lunch, I hope.'

'I can get you something on the way back if you like,' said West, keen to prolong her winning streak. 'I see there's a sushi place on the high street.'

Munro, cringing at the suggestion, regarded her with a look normally reserved for Celtic losing a home game.

'Sushi?' he said. 'Are you joking me?'

'What's wrong with Sushi?' said West. 'It's healthy, fresh, and it's good for you.'

'You think so, Charlie? Are you not aware that that little piece of raw fish, wrapped in seaweed with a dollop of rice, is laced with MSG? And corn syrup, not to mention potassium sorbate and a handful of artificial colours which not only make the dish look pretty, but will also make you hyperactive and quite possibly cause a tumour or two?'

'Oh, and I imagine you'd probably prefer a couple of steak pies, instead?' said West, pushing her luck. 'Or something deep-fried, perhaps?'

Munro's smile unnerved her.

'Oh aye! Perfect, lassie,' he said quietly. 'Tell you what, why not wait until I get back and we'll visit The Duke instead, get blootered on a few pints of Deuchars, then head to the bookies for a wee bet before a haggis supper. What do you say?'

'Sorry. I mean…'

'Cheese and tomato, please. White bread. No butter.'

* * *

The Duke, formerly 'of Edinburgh', was crammed with oversized buggies, screaming toddlers, and mothers enjoying a fixed price lunch consisting mainly of hand-cut, twice-cooked chips served in bo-ho hip, enamelled mugs bought as a job lot from a camping store. West made for the bar, ordered a large vodka, straight up, no ice, and downed it in one. The barman, scraping six feet tall, raised his eyebrows as she ordered another.

'Tough morning?' he quipped, scratching the stubble on his chin.

West, saying nothing, produced her warrant card and flashed it in front of his face.

'Oops. Hope it wasn't too gruesome,' he said, smirking.

She scowled. Her eyes locked on his.

'How old are you?' she snarled.

'Nineteen.'

'Ever been in trouble, son?' she said.

'Me? Course not!' he said nervously.

'Well, play your cards right, and you might be.'

CHAPTER 5

"WHAT WAS SHE LIKE?"

San Francisco. Mellow, congenial, alluring, a little old-fashioned and built on a fault. Not as temperamental as the San Andreas, perhaps, but just as volatile and liable to crumble at any moment. Like I say, despite her outward appearance, her public persona, you know – confident, self-assured and fiercely independent – underneath it all, she was actually quite fragile. Underneath it all, she was still the little girl who'd just lost her father. All she really wanted was for someone to guide her, someone to tell her what to do. She wanted to be held, to feel safe. Protected. I'd wrap her in my arms and she'd snuggle in, tight, like a puppy craving warmth and, more often than not, fall asleep. It gave me a sense of purpose, I think. Made me feel as though it were my duty to shield her from harm.

There was an aura of unsullied innocence about her, like the proverbial girl next door, enhanced by the fact that she was free from artificial additives. No lipstick, no blusher, no mascara, no nothing. Plain and simple, just as nature intended. Her hair was neither blonde nor brown, it was that in-between shade. I suppose you could have called it either, depending on the light. She wore it short, shorter than a bob; said it was practical. Low maintenance. With her big green eyes and little pointed chin, she looked like a pixie, a mischievous sprite, which, all things considered, was quite appropriate. She had, shall we say, a slightly twisted, almost impish idea of fun.

She thought nothing of dropping little notes through letterboxes chosen at random, most often on her way to work. Little notes, written with a fountain pen on vellum paper and sealed in plain envelopes. Notes which read 'I know where you live', 'Let's meet again', 'Keep your doors locked' or 'I miss you'. I could almost hear the ensuing arguments, the threat of divorce lawyers and the sound of suitcases hitting the pavement.

Harry also fell victim, soon after they met. He'd just opened the bar, he was still drinking, and she could see he needed help. However, what she thought was funny almost broke him in two. It was, by any standards, creepy. It didn't take long for her to acquire a set of keys to his flat – in his perpetual state of inebriation he didn't even notice they were missing. They'd known each other seventy-two hours, it was four in the morning and Harry, out for the count, didn't hear the door open. She'd gone there with the intention of moving the furniture around, just little things, enough to make him stop and think, enough to unsettle him, shock him in to giving up the booze, but when she saw how sparsely furnished it was, I mean, a sofa and a coffee table, she had to think again. She found him upstairs. He looked pathetic, sprawled out on the bed, snoring and dribbling like some orphaned waif. She stood in the shadows and watched as his chest, bathed in moonlight, heaved with every audible intake of breath. His phone, face down on the floor beside him, glowed softly with unanswered calls. She picked it up, took a single picture of his troubled face, and left. Come the morning, or what was left of it, he checked his phone and, apart from the shock of seeing an alcoholic in his bed, assumed he must have taken it himself. He trashed it, went to work, and forgot about it. Until the following morning. He checked his phone. Same alcoholic. Different photo. Six days later, he was a paranoid wreck who'd taken to sleeping with a hammer under the bed. That's when he gave up drinking.

I was lucky, I escaped with my mind intact. My body, however, was not so fortunate. Play fighting was something she enjoyed with vigour. According to her rules, biting and scratching were allowed, which invariably left me bleeding from wounds surrounded by teeth marks. She assaulted my taste buds, on more than one occasion, by substituting the salt for sugar, and vice-versa, then collapsing in a fit of uncontrollable giggles as I spat out French fries which had been unnecessarily sweetened or tea which was nothing more than a warm, saline solution. Relaxing on the sofa was best approached with a degree of caution too, lest my derriere be speared by the copious amounts of cocktail sticks she'd stuck deep within the cushion.

She was clever, no doubt about it; I mean you'd have to be to come up with pranks like that. Maybe that's why she got on so well with Harry, maybe that's why their relationship was more cerebral than physical. She was modest about it, though; never mouthed off, never said 'actually, you're wrong, the correct answer is…'. She knew she had nothing to prove. Sometimes, of a Sunday evening for example, she'd sit quietly and rattle through a crossword as though it were a tedious chore, frustrated by the simplicity of the clues. Given the opportunity, she preferred to use her God-given talent for planning and deception to exercise the old grey matter by playing chess, for example. Unfortunately, I was not a worthy opponent. The words 'check' and 'mate' spilled from her lips with alarming speed each time we played.

She liked her job. At first, I thought it was below her; I thought was she was wasting her talents. I mean, working in the archive department couldn't have been that taxing.

File this, number that. I thought she'd have been more suited to something that would make her brain hurt, like stem cell research, or... or, I don't know, finding a new molecular compound. But it soon dawned on me that it satisfied her craving for regimen and order. For want of a better word, her OCD.

Take her house – the stuff in her house – it was neat and tidy, yes, but excessively so. Everything lined up, everything was straight. For example, open any drawer in the chest of drawers in the bedroom and you'll find all her socks arranged in rows, on a single level, organised by length and colour. Same with the underwear. And the jumpers. And the tee-shirts and the vests. The stuff in the wardrobe is hung according to length and grouped by use, coats on the left, then the cardigans, then the shirts, and at the bottom, her shoes. I say shoes, they were trainers – that's all she wore, each pair in a transparent plastic box marked with the date she bought them. The kitchen was the same, as was the bathroom, and the lounge. Now, I know what you're thinking, that she was just house-proud and it really isn't that unusual, but it went further than that. It was the way she approached things mentally, as well.

I suppose the first time I noticed it, this obsession for order, that is, was when she invited me to dinner. Not a take-away, not an impulsive affair simply because we were hungry, but a proper meal, one which she'd prepared. We had sirloin. The plates were square and set in perfect alignment with the grid on the checked tablecloth, as was the cutlery. The steaks, cooked black and blue, had been trimmed so they, too, were square, and surrounding them were twelve, perfectly aligned, homemade chips, cut from spuds she'd grown at her small allotment. Three to the left, three to the right, three to the top and three beneath. All cut to fit. That wasn't just to make the plate look pretty; I'm telling you, it had nothing to do with aesthetics.

Then there's the other thing. The numbers. I washed the dishes, as any guest would, and, in clearing them away, it hit me. Three. She had a thing about the number three. She had three plates, three knives and three forks. There was a spare chair at the table. There were three cushions on the sofa. The books on the shelves were arranged in blocks of three, separated by vases or picture frames, marble Buddhas or candles. I looked at her glass, vodka and tomato juice, three ice cubes bobbing on the top. Naturally, I asked why. I had to. The third-eye, or the sixth chakra, I was told, is the gateway to the inner self, the vehicle that will take you on a journey of enlightenment to a place of higher consciousness. The sixth chakra enables you to merge intuition with rational thought, a primeval instinct long since buried by our reliance on the trappings of modern life. I felt foolish. I should've known.

It obviously worked for her, whatever it was — the belief, the lifestyle — she was so... balanced. So in-tune with her surroundings. She's probably the only person I have ever met who wasn't prone to mood swings. She never got angry; nothing irritated her.

Unlike Howard Hughes, her compulsive behaviour didn't stretch to excessive cleaning, disposing of toothbrushes after a single use, or a morbid fear of germs. On the contrary, if the occasion called for it, she rather enjoyed getting 'messy', particularly if it involved flesh. Skinning it, gutting it, ripping the innards out and hacking it to pieces. As a child, she took great comfort in the rabbit stew her mother used to make and, sometime into the third week of our 'dalliance', she proudly announced I was to partake in her memory of it. I was flattered, only because I took it as a veiled invitation to visit the oddly named Winnersh. Sadly, the invitation was not forthcoming, she was to cook the stew herself. Even better, I thought. Nothing worse than standing on ceremony while prospective in-laws conducted a vetting process based entirely on appearance, wealth and manners. I assumed, however, she'd get the rabbit from the butcher, or the supermarket, nicely portioned up as unidentifiable joints of something resembling a chicken. But no. I arrived at her place to find Thumper lying on the kitchen table, looking, to all intents and purposes, as though he were asleep. The urge to retire to the other room was almost overwhelming but I felt obliged to sit and watch the spectacle unfold. She only used the carving knife once, to separate his head from the body. Then she produced a paring knife and, holding it like a pen, as one would when performing an autopsy, I imagine, she sliced him open and teased the skin from the flesh. She wasn't rough, didn't tug or heave, she was gentle. It was like watching her undress a favourite doll. The sound was the worst thing, like a silk sheet being ripped in two. Anyway, once he was naked, any association with Watership Down vanished into thin air. Out came the guts – she wasn't one for offal – and within a couple of minutes, the poor fella was boned and jointed. I declined the offer of his foot, for luck. It obviously hadn't worked for him.

Other gifts, of which there were plenty, I accepted graciously. Nothing fancy, nothing bought from a shop, just stuff she'd found or picked up along the way, but each one presented with a product of her vividly fertile imagination. The pebble shaped like a heart, for example, wasn't just a pebble. It was proof that the man who turned to stone on hearing of his beloved's demise, actually existed. The dry-cleaning ticket had been dropped by a bridesmaid who, as a consequence, was unable to retrieve her dress from the cleaners and thereby missed the wedding but found love with the shop assistant. The Victorian key with a filigree bow, cast in brass, would open a chest containing the Holy Grail, buried beneath the mountains of Puglia. And then, there was the scalpel. One of her scalpels. An integral part of the artist's toolbox, she said, as essential as a sable brush. It was the only gift that didn't come wrapped in a fable. I thought nothing of it. Never occurred to me that she used them too. Not in the way an artist would. More a surgeon. And that, I suppose, was her negative side.

CHAPTER 6

SPRATT HALL ROAD, WANSTEAD. 3:32pm
Munro, framed by the doorway, stood perfectly still, cocked his head to one side and regarded the drowsy detective with a look of bemusement.

'Are we keeping you up?' he said sternly.

West woke with a jolt, her hands unable to decide whether to fix her hair or fiddle with the laptop.

'I…'

'This is not Madrid, Charlie. We don't do siestas here.'

'I know,' said West. 'I must have… you're late.'

'Indeed, I am.'

'I thought it was just a sentencing…'

'As did I,' said Munro, taking a seat. 'The defence, however, did not. In lieu of some staggering new evidence, no doubt purporting the accused to be mentally unstable or under the influence of some mind-altering substance, they have lodged an appeal. Sentencing has subsequently been postponed until the twenty-third.'

'I see. Oh, well,' said West. 'On the bright side, I got you a sandwich.'

'Very kind, I'm sure. And how was your sushi?'

'Sorry?'

41

'Your sushi?' said Munro.

'Oh. Nice,' said West. 'Actually, I had sashimi.'

'Is that a fact? And they make sashimi with pastry now?'

West looked flummoxed.

'You've crumbs. Down your front,' said Munro.

West, rattled by his irritatingly astute observation, dusted off the remnants of a sausage roll and made for the kettle.

'So. Progress, Charlie?' said Munro. 'Have you made any?'

'Sir. DVLA. He's got a Land Rover Defender. Registered in his name but to his parents' address. We found it in the car park. Forensics are on it now.'

'Good,' said Munro, eyeing the wilting sandwich with distaste. 'And our part-time P.C., did he obtain a description of the girl from the fellow across the way?'

'Yes. Vague, but it's something. She was short, slightly built, wearing a thick woolly cardigan-type-thing and a knitted cap.'

'And that's it?'

''Fraid so. Told you it was vague. Claims he hardly saw her face.'

'Oh, well. How about…'

'The phone?'

'Aye, the phone,' said Munro.

'Sergeant Cole took it to "Inta" this morning, in Greenwich. As it happens, he's on his way back now, but I doubt we'll get anywhere with it.'

'And why would that be?' said Munro.

'No sim card,' said West assuredly. 'Whoever put the phone there, removed the sim.'

Munro, weary from the wasted trip to court, held his head in hands and sighed.

'Oh, lassie,' he said, 'lassie, lassie, lassie. And I thought the younger generation were up on all this technology stuff. I'd brush up if I were you, assuming you want to keep "detective" as a part of your job title.'

'What do you mean?' said West, defensively. 'If there's no sim, then...'

'Then, there's no problem,' said Munro. 'Look, let's say you save all your precious bits of information, your contacts and your photos and your emails and such, to your sim card; you think it's safe, don't you? And you think that when you take your sim card out, all your information goes with you. Am I right?'

'Well, yes.'

'Well, no, Charlie. No. When you save all that nonsense to the sim, your phone, your clever, wee smartphone, is so clever, it also saves it to the internal memory. Scrambling it, hiding it, stashing it under every digital nook and cranny it can possibly find.'

'What?' said West, genuinely surprised.

'My advice,' said Munro, 'should you ever decide to rid yourself of that intrusive piece of technology, is to do a factory reset before you part with it. Better still, do a reset, and then destroy it.'

West, astounded by Munro's knowledge on the subject, passed him a mug.

'You've not eaten your sandwich,' she said.

'No. I... I had a wee something at the court,' said Munro, sipping his tea. 'Perhaps later. So, what else?'

West returned to her desk, opened her notebook and did her best to look proficient.

'Footprints,' she said. 'One thing a wooden floor is good for, is picking up prints. Now, discarding ours, and those we assume belong to Farnsworth-Brown, SOCO found one other set of latent prints. Rubber soles. He recognised them straight away. Converse. Ladies, size 5. She's heavy on her left foot, the heel's worn down more than the right.'

'And what makes you think they're of any significance?' said Munro, eyeing her as if she were on trial.

'Well, I... for a start,' she said hesitantly, fearful of making a fool of herself, 'the size, size 5, that could match the girl seen with Farnsworth-Brown. On the stairs. Based on height and build, that is.'

'Go on.'

'And they ran from the door, the front door, one set, straight up the staircase to where we found the phone, and out again. That indicates she knew where she was going.'

'I see,' said Munro.

'So, my hunch is, and I'm not saying I'm right, but my hunch is that the prints belong to that girl, the one on the stairwell, and she was the one who cleaned the phone, swiped the sim and placed it by the bed.'

Munro leaned back in his chair and folded his arms, one hand beneath his chin.

'These footprints, Charlie, do you not think they could, maybe, belong to the cleaner?' he said quietly.

'What? The cleaner?' said West anxiously.

'Well, the flat was spotless,' said Munro. 'As you know, the entire place had been scrubbed from top to bottom. Now, if you're a cleaner, I'd say those Converse would be a sensible choice of footwear, comfortable and practical, especially if you're on your feet all day.'

'I hadn't... that means...'

'Perhaps those footprints have nothing to do with the girl or the phone.'

'Shit. Sorry,' said West, dejected. 'It was just a hunch...'

'Charlie!' said Munro, pounding the desk. 'Where's your confidence? We don't even know if he has a cleaner and if he does, why did we not find her fingerprints around the rest of the flat? Well done, lassie. I think. So, come on, what do we do next?'

'Erm, we, we look for the girl?'

'Good. And where would we start?'

'I'm not... Clock Court. Cameras. Of course, CCTV. It's a private complex, they must have...'

'Off you go.'

* * *

Sergeant Cole, as subtle as the battering ram he employed so efficiently, knocked once and flew through the door without waiting for a response.

'Guv,' he said, grinning.

'Tommy! As gentle as Katrina on the banks of the Mississippi. You're looking pleased with yourself.'

'It's the lads at Inta, guv, don't know how they do it.'

'Take a seat,' said Munro. 'And you Charlie, you should hear this before you go. What have you got?'

'Hunger pangs,' said Cole.

'Come again?'

'Not eaten, guv. Feeling a bit, you know.'

Munro smiled and gently pushed the sandwich across his desk.

'Be my guest,' he said.

'You sure?' said Cole, ripping the cellophane off the pack. 'Very kind, ta.'

'Charlie,' said Munro, 'let's have a brew. I'm sure Tommy could use one to stop that culinary delight from sticking to his throat.'

'Sir,' said West as she reluctantly filled the kettle.

'So, come on, Tommy, we're all ears.'

'Right, guv. Well, this Harry geezer, so far as his phone's concerned, he wasn't a hefty user, I mean, he didn't download data, didn't browse the internet, didn't do Facebook or any of that stuff.'

'A man after my own heart.'

'Seems he pretty much used the phone as a phone. And a camera.'

Sergeant Cole pulled a memory stick from his pocket and gestured towards West's laptop.

'Miss, could we…'

'Of course,' said West, passing it over.

'Here,' said Cole as the images cascaded down the screen, 'look at these. This one's of a bar, they Googled it

– it's his place in Shoreditch; then there's this girl, half a dozen shots of her. Pretty thing, younger sister, maybe?'

West peered over Munro's shoulder.

'Short. Slightly built,' she said. 'I'd say that's his girlfriend, and could well be the girl we're looking for, sir.'

'No "might be" about it, Charlie,' said Munro. 'Look at her feet. Left ankle. Blue star. Converse.'

'God, you don't miss a trick, do you?'

'No. I do not. Tommy?'

'Guv. Here's where it gets a bit odd. Look, four pics here, all of a bloke sleeping, I'm assuming it's Farnsworth-Brown, cos it looks like his bedroom.'

'Yes,' said West assertively. 'That's him. Selfies. What's odd about that?'

Sergeant Cole glanced at Munro.

'With all due respect, miss,' he said, hesitating. 'They can't be selfies, he's asleep.'

West winced.

'And they were taken on consecutive days, between 3 and 4am.'

Munro stared at the screen, frowning as he scrutinised the photos.

'So,' he mumbled, 'why would someone want to take his picture while he slept?'

'Easy,' said West. 'Girlfriend, again. Men look cute when they're sleeping, it's a girly thing to do. A keepsake.'

'Then why did she not take them on her own phone, so she could keep them?' said Munro, shaking his head. 'And why take them at 3 in the morning? Are they recent?'

'No, guv,' said Sergeant Cole. 'They were taken yonks ago, I mean, couple of years, at least.'

'I see. In that case, they may have no bearing on this investigation at all. Nothing like a red herring to make things a wee bit interesting, eh? Is that it, Tommy?'

'No guv,' said Cole, reaching for his notebook. 'Not by a long chalk. Numbers. For someone who ran a bar he wasn't what you might call sociable. Practical, more like.

46

Dull, even. Dentist, doctor, locksmith, Tiffin Tin, that's the Indian takeaway, Oriental Chef, that's the Chinese, garage in Woodford, bloke called Chris, turns out he's the manager at the bar, and half a dozen numbers for someone called Sheba.'

'Sheba?' said Munro. 'Either royalty or a cat. Why six numbers? Why not the one?'

'Who knows, but I can tell you this, we tried all the numbers on the phone, see, and they're all legit, they all work, except for the ones attributed to Sheba. They're all dead.'

'Dead?'

'They're mobiles. Pay as you go. Every one of them. Each one, a different network.'

Munro stood suddenly, turned towards the window and gazed pensively down towards the green.

'This Sheba,' he said, 'does not want to be traced. She's clever.'

'She?' said Cole.

'Aye. She. The Queen of Sheba. I'm beginning to think Farnsworth-Brown was her Solomon.'

'You've lost me, guv.'

'The Queen of Sheba, Tommy, had everything a girl could want, not just power and a country to rule over but she was clever, too. Clever, beautiful and, above all, mysterious; a bit of an enigma, you might say. She was drawn to Solomon, not for his wealth, but for his mind. He was wise beyond his years, a gift bestowed upon him by God himself. He had the answer to everything.'

'Right,' said Cole, shrugging his shoulders. 'So, you're saying this Farnsworth-Brown was a bit of an intellectual?'

'It's possible.'

'And this Sheba, she was kind of his muse?'

'Other way round, I think, Tommy. What was the last call he made?'

Sergeant Cole glanced at his notebook.

'Er, last call he made was to… Oriental Chef. Takeaway.'

'What?' said Munro, turning on his heels. 'Not her? Not Sheba?'

'Nope. All the calls logged as Sheba were incoming. And the last time she called him was six days ago, last Thursday at 6:22pm.'

'Charlie,' said Munro excitedly, 'when did that nice Scottish gentleman say he saw him last?'

'Erm…'

'Quick, Charlie, come on, I've no time for dawdlers.'

'Checking,' said West, frantically flicking through her notebook. 'I'm checking, here it is, according to the chimp…'

'Detective Sergeant West,' said Munro, raising his voice, 'the term is PCSO. I'll not have derogatory slang in my office, do I make myself clear?'

'Sir,' said West, recoiling. 'According to the PCSO, they passed on the stairs… oh, last Thursday. About half six, he said, quarter to seven.'

'Tommy. GPS. Did he have his phone with him last Thursday?'

'No, guv. It was at his place.'

'Damn. Did they find any other locations on the phone, any residential addresses?'

'Nope. He was about as adventurous as his social life. Creature of habit. Flitted between his house and Shoreditch.'

'Maybe he turned his phone off a lot,' ventured West. 'Save batteries, that's why there's nothing from the GPS?'

'Nice try, Charlie,' said Munro. 'but here's another nugget for you to squirrel away. Your smartphone, even when it's switched off and the GPS isn't active, "pings" the phone masts every seven seconds, or thereabouts, which means we can tell, roughly, where you are, or where you've been. However, with the phone on and the GPS enabled, we can pinpoint you – track you, even – to within a couple of metres.'

'You are joking? But that's invasion of privacy, why isn't this public knowledge?'

'Oh, but it is, lassie. You just have to know where to find it.'

'So,' said West. 'What do we do now? Appeal, posters, that kind of thing?'

'No, no, no,' said Munro, agitated. 'It's too soon. No, we'll wait. 48 hours. We'll wait.'

He turned to the window, hands clasped behind his back, and stared blankly into space.

'There has to be someone else,' he muttered. 'A fellow doesn't run a bar and live like a hermit; it's a sociable occupation. There must be someone else we should be talking to. Charlie, when are his folks due back?'

'Today, no yesterday, or was it tomorrow. I can check, hold on.'

'Och, Charlie, you're trying my patience, you know that? Give Sergeant Cole the number. Tommy, wee favour please, find out when they're back, quick as you can.'

'Guv.'

'Now, Charlie, where do they live?'

'Erm, Abingdon. I think.'

'You think?'

'I know,' said West, cringing. 'I mean, I know. Abingdon. Near Oxford.'

'Excellent,' said Munro. 'It's not far. Wee trip up the A40, be there in no time.'

'They're home, guv,' said Tommy. 'Landed this morning.'

'Good. Right, lassie, get going. It's late.'

West grabbed her coat and bag.

'Sir. Clock Court,' she said. 'Is it worth coming back once I've had a look?'

'No, no,' said Munro. 'You take yourself off home and get some rest. I want you here early, we're away to Abingdon, first thing.'

* * *

Tired and down-trodden, West stood alone in the car park, her enthusiasm for detecting on the wane. Clock Court, by the eerie glow of the yellow streetlamps, had lost its appeal as a complex of over-priced apartments. It looked, instead, more like the mournful, haunting asylum it once was. She cast an eye around the building, no more than a cursory glance, and concluded, in the absence of any security cameras, that it was time to leave.

* * *

The Duke was doing a brisk trade, packed with thirty-somethings sipping prosecco and deriding the opening of yet another supermarket on the High Street. A familiar figure, wearing a tweed jacket and college scarf, was leaning on the wrong side of the bar. He caught her eye, pushed through the crowd, and walked over.

'This is a pleasant surprise,' he said with a grin. 'Wasn't sure if I was in trouble or not.'

'You are now,' said West brusquely. 'You finished?'

'Yes.'

'Good. Come on.'

'Where to?'

'Shoreditch. I know a nice cosy place we can go.'

CHAPTER 7

"DID YOU KNOW WHAT SHE'D DONE?"
Yes. Of course I knew. Found out by accident, really.
What I mean is, she didn't give me this serious look one
night and say 'listen, there's something you ought to know,
something I need to tell you'. An opportunity presented
itself and she welcomed it. She was positively beaming, in
fact. Her face, full of excitement. It was like she'd been on
some wonderfully exotic adventure and couldn't wait to
tell me all about it.

We'd finished dinner and I, being the ever-thankful
guest, offered to clear away the dishes, as usual. An offer,
based on my previous efforts, which she politely declined
for no other reason that, in her eyes, I would never be able
to do it right. It simply wasn't in me to keep count of how
many wipes of the sponge I made, or whether I was doing
it in a clockwise direction, let alone knowing exactly where
in the cupboards everything lived, so I poured us some
more wine, left her to it and went to the lounge.

There's a side table, just inside the door, where she kept
an old anglepoise lamp and a box. I accidentally knocked it
as I brushed by. No big deal, it hardly moved, but the box
was out of true – didn't line up with the edge of the table

anymore – so I thought I'd better straighten it up before she came in. It was a cigar box, wooden, with 'Cohiba' on the top, 'Cohiba Siglo No.1'. A Siglo's a small cigar, not one of those ridiculously large things that Hollywood would have you believe everyone on Wall Street smokes. Anyway, I straightened the box, made sure it was square with the table, and that's when I realised it wasn't empty. Well, curiosity got the better of me. I had a feeling there wouldn't be any cigars in it, if anything, I was expecting it to house all manner of knick-knacks; you know – cotton reels, loose change, matches, an old biro or a couple of theatre tickets, that sort of thing. So I released the little brass catch and opened it up. I didn't think they were real at first, I thought they were edible; sweets made from sugar, the kind of thing you'd buy at the seaside; or something she'd bought from a joke shop; after all, with her sense of humour, it wouldn't have surprised me. I mean, no-one keeps fingers in a cigar box, do they? I mean, real fingers? Human fingers? Eight of them, all individually wrapped in clear, airtight bags. I was transfixed, intrigued. I contemplated giving them a gentle nudge, a prod, to see what they felt like, when in she walked. She didn't shout or close the box or even question why I had my nose in her personal belongings, she just grinned and said something like 'oh, you've found my souvenirs, then'. Souvenirs? Must have been one hell of a holiday, I thought.

She sat beside me on the floor. I knew what was coming. Another tingle. It was like listening to a fairy-tale, not a first-hand description of body disposal. I'd be lying if I said I wasn't... concerned; if I didn't think that I might be next. Fact is, I was so engrossed, I really didn't care.

He was, in her words, 'no-one important', just some chap she'd met by chance. They'd been out together a couple of times. He was okay at first; genial, polite – they got on well. He knew lots of stuff about everything, one of society's intelligentsia, but it wasn't long before he showed his true colours and things turned sour. He wasn't violent, or abusive, not in the physical sense. He was stubborn, pig-headed. A control freak. He got on her nerves, telling her what she should eat, commenting on her wardrobe and berating her for being late; so she finished it. Don't blame her, all that after a couple of dates, I'd have done the same. I know now that what she said wasn't strictly true, it wasn't just a couple of weeks, nor was it just a couple of dates, but it doesn't matter now. I'm not going to hold it against her. Anyway, he must have had selective hearing because, despite being told to piss off, he kept hounding her, demanding to know why she wasn't at his beck and call; so she relented. Agreed to see him one more time. Sort things out for good. They met at his place. As usual, he'd made no effort to smarten himself up, didn't even bother to take her coat when she arrived. The first thing he said when he opened the door was 'did you bring food? I'm hungry'. He was what you might call a bit of a slob. A rich, lazy, misogynistic slob. Fortunately, she'd gone prepared – a couple of bottles of Rioja and some chorizo. They sat and talked, about him mainly, about how hard he worked and how she should show him a little more respect because he was so wealthy. Red rag. Bull. He turned his nose up at the wine, wasn't used to drinking, apparently, but in the absence of anything else, she finally coaxed him into it, and he dived right in. She was laughing when she told me about it; said she'd never seen anyone so tipsy after a single glass – he was practically hammered. Didn't stop him polishing off the second bottle, though. On his own. After which, he collapsed on the sofa and passed out; which was, conveniently, exactly what she had planned – had hoped would happen.

She unpacked her bag while he slept. Ground sheets, disposable decorator's overalls, rubber gloves, airtight storage bags and the cigar box. She pulled on the overalls, spread the ground sheets over the floor and fetched a bucket from under the sink. She took a Vacutainer needle from the cigar box – it's one of those needles they use when you give a blood sample – but instead of attaching a vial to collect a sample, she attached a plastic hose and stuck the other end in the bucket. He was out cold; didn't even feel the needle go in. Brachial artery. Upper arm. Just above the elbow. Then out it flowed. Ten and a half pints of Type O. Took just over a minute. That's all. Just over a minute to drain the very life from his body. He went peacefully, I mean, he was none the wiser. Just faded away, blissfully unaware that his trip to the land of nod was one-way only.

The blood was flushed down the toilet bowl, followed by an entire bottle of bleach. Then out came the scalpel. I always thought you'd need something like a chainsaw to chop up a corpse, but not so. She borrowed a bread knife from the kitchen but apart from that, she did it all with that scalpel. Amazing really. He wasn't all bad, she'd said; it wasn't his fault he was a complete arse. He'd had his good points. His hands. He had nice hands. Unfortunately, all they were good for, once she'd finished, was giving the thumbs-up. She was there for hours. Patiently, methodically, painstakingly taking him apart, joint by joint, bagging up the bits as she went. The feet, the lower legs, the knees, the thighs, his pelvis, his hands – what was left of them – lower arms, upper arms, his head, his big head, and his torso. That was the only bit which gave her grief, thanks to his 48" chest. She said it was like trying to stuff a duvet back in the bag it came in, but she managed, eventually. There was a look of smug satisfaction on her face, a naughty twinkle in her eye, when she told me he looked like a kit of parts, waiting to be reassembled with a tube of glue and a couple of stitches. I don't know what she did with him, unless she's got some bloody big cigar boxes somewhere. I mean, what do you do with stuff like that? Everything else, the ground sheets, overalls, his clothes, even the bucket, she took to her allotment and burned them in the incinerator. Probably on the rhubarb now, I expect.

CHAPTER 8

ARNOLD CIRCUS, SHOREDITCH. 6:52am
West, resisting the urge to open her eyes, moaned as a
pneumatic drill pounded the back of her head. She rolled
over, blocking the harsh, morning sun from her face and
stretched out an arm. The sheets beside her were rumpled
and bare. The pillow, hollowed out where a head had lain,
reeked of pomade. She sat up and listened for the shower
running, the toilet flushing or the tinkle of a spoon in a
coffee cup. There was nothing. The flat was still. Relieved
that she was alone, she fell from the bed, picked herself up
and stumbled to the kitchen. Her stomach churned in
disgust at the lingering stench of chilli sauce and raw onion
and the sight of two, half-eaten kebabs, their contents
smeared across the table. An empty bottle of Smirnoff
Blue lay on the draining board. Beside it, a pair of knickers.
She rubbed her eyes, searched half-heartedly for the packet
of paracetamol and flicked the kettle on. The mirror did
not do her any favours. She averted her eyes and almost
gagged as she brushed her teeth. The phone whistled.
Missed call. Time: 7:06am. 'Oh, shit!' she groaned as she
frantically searched for her jeans. 'Shit! shit! shit!' The

kettle reached a bubbling crescendo as the door slammed behind her.

* * *

Munro, as bombproof as a gelding on riot duty, barely flinched as Hurricane Cole burst through the door.

'Blimey, guv, you still here?' he said.

'Aye.'

'Sorry, if I'd known, I'd have knocked. Thought you'd left ages ago.'

'No.'

'No sign of D.S. West, then?'

'No,' said Munro.

'And you're not impressed.'

'I am not.'

'Wonder where she is then. Tea?'

'Yes, please,' said Munro.

'Maybe the alarm didn't go off.'

'Then she needs to buy a new one.'

'Maybe there's delays,' said Cole. 'On the tube, like.'

'Then she should take a taxi.'

'Do you want me to give her a bell?'

'No, no. No doubt she'll surface as soon as the fog clears.'

'Fog?' said Cole. 'You've lost me.'

'I'll not cast aspersions, Tommy, not until I'm sure. Let's just say, I think there's something a wee bit, intoxicating, about Detective Sergeant West.'

Cole grinned.

'You're not wrong there, guv,' he said. 'She's a bit...'

'Attractive,' said Munro with a timely interruption. 'I think you'll find the word you're looking for, Tommy, is attractive.'

'Almost.'

West crept quietly up the last few steps and paused outside the door. Her heart was racing, her hands, clammy.

She took a deep breath and tried desperately to compose herself.

'I'm so sorry,' she said as she entered the office. 'I had a terrible... the traffic was...'

'Good Lord,' said Cole. 'I mean, morning, miss.'

Munro looked on, astounded by her appearance.

'Sleep well, Charlie?' he said, squinting, his head cocked to one side.

'Well, yes, I think so...'

'Was it not a wee bit... uncomfortable?'

'Sir?'

'Lying with your head amongst those bricks, surrounded by...?'

'I don't know what you...'

'You look like you've slept in a skip, lassie,' said Munro. 'You're as white as a sheet. And you're late. Incredibly, unacceptably, late.'

'Sorry, I can explain,' said West, flustered. 'You see, what happened was...'

'Och, stop your havering, I'm not interested. Tommy, do her a coffee, would you. Black. Strong.'

'I'm fine, really,' said West. 'I just...'

'Haud your wheesht,' said Munro, raising an accusing finger. 'Now, you listen to me, lassie. This time, I'll let it go. There'll be no warning the next. Do you understand?'

'Sir.'

'Good. Now, drink that and tell me about last night.'

West almost dropped her cup.

'Last night?' she said, alarmed by the request. 'Why do you need to...'

'The cameras, Charlie! Good God, has your memory gone as well as your self-esteem?'

'Cameras? Oh Christ, yes, the cameras. Of course. There aren't any. I checked. Their security leaves a lot to be desired.'

'It's not the only thing.'

'I looked everywhere,' said West, cradling the coffee, 'all around the building, I even checked the street, Hermon Hill, to see if there were any traffic cameras which might have caught her, but I'm afraid…'

Munro cut her short.

'Tommy, we're taking the "Q" car,' he said, pulling on his coat. 'That way we can make up for lost time. Call his bank for me, get copies of his statements, I want to know if there's been any activity on his accounts, cash withdrawals in particular.'

'Guv.'

'You,' he said, scowling at West. 'Let's go.'

* * *

Munro adjusted his seat and mirrors, buckled up and instructed West to enter the postcode on the sat nav before she passed out. She rifled through her bag, cursing as she searched for her notebook.

'Listen, Charlie,' he said, softly. 'I'm not one to pry, but if you're having problems, let me know, now. I can't afford to carry dead wood. Do you need some time off?'

West slumped in her seat.

'No,' she said, heaving a sigh. 'Just a rough night. I'm sorry. Won't happen again.'

'Okay, then. I'll take your word for it.'

'Thanks. So, are they expecting us?'

'Expecting us?' said Munro. 'Why, no, Charlie, of course not.'

'But… but what if they're out?'

'Then we'll wait.'

'But they may be…'

'Listen, lassie, if someone's expecting a call from the police, they will, without doubt, pre-empt the questions, mull them over and then concoct a fistful of answers and alibis that have no bearing on the truth. No matter how innocent they are. Trust me. You'll not get a straight answer. Ever. Now, get your head down. I'll nudge you when we're there.'

* * *

Munro eased the car gently down the gravel drive and parked by the old stable block, a few yards short of the front door. He peered through the windscreen and cast an envious eye over the rambling pile. Built from rich, golden Cotswold stone, it was quintessentially English, irrefutably rural and, undoubtedly, unaffordable.

A middle-aged woman, as plump as a Christmas turkey with rosy cheeks and an apron bound tightly around her ample waist, answered the door and regarded Munro suspiciously.

'Yes?' she said.

'Mrs Farnsworth-Brown?' asked Munro.

'No.'

'I thought not. Would you be so kind as to tell her I'm here. If it's not too much trouble, that is.'

'And who shall I say is calling?'

Munro held up his warrant card.

'Oh. Shan't be a tick,' she said, scurrying away.

Munro glanced back at Detective Sergeant West, dozing in the car. There was something about her that reminded him of Christy MacAdam. It wasn't so much the colour of her hair, nor was it the blanched skin, it was the way her head lolled lifelessly to one side, her eyes closed, her mouth agape. They found Christy in the same position, in the car park behind The Annandale Arms; only difference was, he'd been shot. Point blank. Straight through the head. Munro's eyes glazed over.

* * *

Christy MacAdam. Forty-eight years old, twenty-two stone, 6'4", 90% blubber. He was so fat, his coat was worn where the steering wheel had rubbed against his belly. He'd moved from Stranraer to Lochside, lived alone and had never worked a day in his life. His undeclared source of income came from pushing smack, his forte, weaning the kids off cannabis and coke until they were hooked on the hard stuff, then fleecing them for everything they had. And when they couldn't pay for their fix, he used them as runners, decoys, prostitutes and rent boys. They were easily, but foolishly, intimidated by his size. In reality, MacAdam was about as agile as a bull elephant with rigor mortis. He wheezed when he walked, coughed when he talked, and slept on the sofa because he couldn't make it up the stairs. Munro had spent precisely eleven months, two weeks and five days, watching, tracking, tailing, logging and recording his every move, compiling a watertight case before hauling him into court. The evidence was overwhelming. There was no dispute. MacAdam, despite entering a plea of not guilty, went down for twelve years. He was out in three. Out in three with a score to settle.

Munro was in his office, first floor, Cornwall Mount, when he took the call. It was 8.32pm. He thought it was Jean, ringing to scold him for being late. He left immediately. Despite the crowd, comprising neighbours and other familiar faces, there wasn't much to look at, just smouldering roof timbers and blackened windows. Jean had already been taken to the infirmary. She didn't last long, not at her age. The smoke took her down, swiftly and gently, so said the paramedics. She'd have passed out before she knew what was happening. Munro took what solace he could from the meaningless statement. Another few months and they'd have been in Carsethorn, by the sea, shivering and holding hands along the beach. It wasn't what he'd expected. Nor was the forensic analysis. The fire wasn't caused by the chip-pan catching fire, nor was it the dodgy switch by the immersion heater which flickered of its own accord, shorting out. It was arson. The accelerant was diesel and so, coincidentally, was MacAdam's car.

Munro, on compassionate leave, spent his time wisely, tailing MacAdam from scheme to scheme, from pub to pub, from bookie to bookie, until finally, *finally*, he got his chance. The car park at the rear of The Annandale Arms. 11.15pm. He'd waited in the shadows until MacAdam, unsteady on his feet, had waddled from the pub and squeezed his bulk behind the wheel, then he pounced, snatching the keys from the ignition before casually, silently, taking a seat on the passenger side. MacAdam laughed. Nervously. He knew he couldn't move, so instead he blethered like a man on the gallows, wheezing and sweating, riled by the fact that Munro stayed silent, uttering not a single, solitary word. The last thing he said simply confirmed what Munro already knew. 'It's chilly out, Inspector, take yourself home, I hear it's nice and warm there.' Munro opened the glove compartment with a flick of the wrist and retrieved the Baikal '79 MacAdam kept hidden there. The pistol was small and light, a couple of pounds at most, but accurate enough, and big enough, to scare the shite out of anyone who stepped out of line. Munro calmly raised the gun, pressed it firmly against MacAdam's perspiring forehead, just above his eyes, and gently squeezed the trigger. 'Not so hard now, are you, big man?' he said.

* * *

'This way, if you please,' said the woman in the apron. 'Follow me.'

'Charlie!' yelled Munro, startled by the intrusion.

West woke with a start, banged her head on the roof, and tumbled from the car.

'An Inspector, I believe?' said Mrs Farnsworth-Brown, holding out her hand.

'Indeed, madam. Detective Inspector Munro. This is Detective Sergeant West.'

'How exciting! Do call me Clarissa, the surname's such a mouthful. This is my husband, Ed.'

'Inspector,' said Ed. 'That's a hell of an accent you have there, Scotland, if I'm not mistaken?'

'Thereabouts, yes.'

'Won't you sit down?' said Clarissa, frowning as she looked at West. 'Are you alright, dear? You look awfully pale.'

'I'm fine, thanks,' said West, forcing a smile. 'Car journeys. I get a bit queasy.'

'I'll fetch you some water. Inspector? Tea? Coffee?'

'Very kind, but no, thank you,' said Munro. 'Just a few questions, if you don't mind.'

'About Harry?' said Ed. 'They said you guys had been asking about him. Don't know what all the fuss is about, he's disappeared before, he's a grown man, he can look after himself.'

'Och, I'm sure you're right,' said Munro. 'But as his staff have raised a concern, I'm afraid we're duty bound to look into it.'

'If you say so,' said Ed. 'Come on, sit.'

'Thanks,' said West as she perched on the edge of the sofa. 'Beautiful house.'

'Thank you,' said Clarissa. '16th century. Some of it, anyway.'

'What was it beforehand? A farm?'

'A dairy, dear,' said Clarissa. 'That's why it's called, "The Old Dairy".'

Ed grinned, tickled by his wife's very British sense of humour.

'So, Inspector,' he said, 'someone thinks Harry's absconded with the takings from the bar?'

Munro stood with his back to the inglenook, hands clasped behind his back.

'Something like that,' he said, smiling. 'It appears some folk, the bar staff, to be precise, are concerned by his absenteeism. Out of character, they say. Oh, I'm sure it's just a hoo-hah over nothing but we'd like to track him down all the same. They're fretting about ordering stock, you know how it is.'

'Oh, sure,' said Ed, laughing. 'Probably wondering how to pay for it, too.'

'Aye, probably. So, can you tell me anything about his friends? Is there anyone he might have contacted to say he was going away?'

Clarissa laughed as she sat next to West.

'Fat chance, Inspector,' she said. 'Harry isn't big on friends, he's never been the sociable type, keeps himself to himself. We only hear from him when he wants something. He's what those people on the news would call "a loner", as if he were some kind of misfit.'

'And was he? I mean, is he?' said Munro.

'Not really. Let's just say he prefers his own company, that's all. He's not very patient, doesn't suffer fools.'

'That's not to say he doesn't know any,' said Ed. 'No. Harry's okay, an introverted extrovert, that's him. Has been ever since he lost Annabel.'

'Annabel?' said Munro, curiously. 'And who might she be?'

'His wife,' said Clarissa, mournfully. 'Lovely girl, so vibrant, so, vivacious. Broke his heart, I think.'

'She left him?' said West, pulling her notebook from her bag.

'She died,' said Ed. 'Such a waste. So young, too.'

'Died?' said Munro.

'Yes. It was a long time ago,' said Clarissa. 'They'd married young. He, twenty-four; she, just out of university. Had a glittering career ahead of her, wanted to be a scientist or something. They were in Aldeburgh.'

'Aldeburgh? That's Suffolk, I know it,' said West. 'It's lovely there, the beach and all.'

'Yes, they were there for the festival,' said Clarissa. 'You know, all that classical music, and the fish and chips, of course. Anyway, she went missing. Harry was beside himself. Said it was his fault, that they'd argued over something, something petty. Always is, isn't it?'

'And then?'

'She stormed off. He didn't go after her, he thought it best she had some space to let off steam, calm down, so to speak. He gave it a couple hours, then a couple more, but by nightfall, he was worried. It was so unlike her, you see. Anyway, he went looking for her. She hadn't taken the car, that was still there, so he traipsed around the village, then down to the beach, thought he'd find her there, gazing up at the stars, or sheltering in a fisherman's hut, but all he found were her plimsolls. Then, her bag. Naturally, he called the police right away but sadly, they never did find her.'

'I'm sorry,' said Munro. 'Can't have been easy. For any of you.'

'Even had the coastguard out,' said Ed. 'She was a strong swimmer, too, but it didn't make sense. Not to me, it just didn't add up.'

'How so?'

'Well, she was so... so level-headed; so sensible. Okay, I didn't know her that well, but she didn't strike me as a risk-taker. Not the kind of person who'd jump in the North Sea in the middle of the night.'

'Well, even if she was, the sea's a lady who demands respect. Trust me, I know. The pull of the tide can...'

'The tide was incoming, Inspector.'

Munro paused and looked at Ed.

'Is that so?' he said, contemplating the implications. 'You know, I might like to have a wee chat about this later,' he said. 'If you don't mind going over...'

'Be happy to, Inspector. Anyway, as Clarissa said, they never found her. Recorded a verdict of misadventure and that's when Harry... that's when Harry hit the bottle.'

'I see,' said Munro. 'If you don't mind me asking, would you happen to know what it was they argued about?'

'The usual,' said Clarissa. 'Ex-girlfriend. She was at the festival too, sheer coincidence, as it happens, but Harry said Annabel was like a woman possessed – furious.

Accused him of having an affair, and them, only just married, too. I think she was a tad insecure.'

'Did you know this girl? The ex-girlfriend?' asked West.

'Vaguely, met her twice, I think,' said Clarissa.

'One of Harry's flings,' said Ed, smiling proudly. 'He sowed so many oats back then you'd think he owned a farm! Didn't last long, few weeks, tops. Sammy was her name, Samantha... Baker, that's it. Baker.'

'They were at university together?' said Munro.

'I assume so. We're lucky if we get a name when Harry brings someone home, let alone their life history.'

'And they didn't keep in touch?'

'Good Lord, no!' said Clarissa, laughing. 'Chalk and cheese, those two. She was too much of a party animal for Harry, he couldn't keep up. Besides, once Annabel came on the scene, he wouldn't have dared. Hell hath no fury, Inspector.'

Munro smiled.

'They looked alike, though,' said Ed. 'Samantha and Annabel, if that helps.'

'In what way?'

'Small. Blondish. Harry has a thing for small chicks.'

'Oh, heavens above, dear,' said Clarissa, 'you're making him sound like some kind of depraved predator. He means petite, Inspector. Harry likes particularly petite girls, brings out the protective side of his nature, I imagine.'

'I see. Well, I'm sure we can find her, should we need to,' he said, nodding at Charlie. 'I'm curious, would you happen to have a photo? Of Annabel, I mean?'

His eyes widened as Clarissa passed him a small silver frame from the mantelpiece. Harry, tall, clean cut and obviously happy, was grinning from ear to ear. He had his arms wrapped around Annabel's shoulders. She was short, fresh-faced and extremely pretty. Her hair, shoulder length, was dark blonde.

'They look like the perfect couple,' said Munro.

'They were, in many ways,' said Clarissa. 'Although I must admit, it did come as bit of a surprise.'

'What did?'

'The wedding of course. I didn't even get to buy a new outfit. They just turned up one day and said they were married. Whirlwind romance, I suppose.'

'So, you hardly knew her?' said Munro.

'That's an understatement, but that's Harry for you,' said Ed with a sigh. 'Mr Impulsive. We joked about it. I said chances are they only got hitched cos they were stoned.'

'And were they?'

'Probably.'

'Would you mind if we borrowed this?' said Munro, passing the frame to West. 'We'll take care of it, naturally; have it back in no time.'

'Of course,' said Clarissa. 'Feel free.'

The conversation paused, temporarily, as Munro, lost in thought, rocked gently back and forth, staring at the flagstones beneath his feet.

'Apologies,' he said bluntly, 'if I sound like I'm straying here, but what was her maiden name? His wife, Annabel?'

'Parkes,' said Clarissa. 'Parkes, with an "e".'

'And was she local, I mean, do you know how they met?'

'No idea, that's another one for Harry, Inspector,' said Clarissa. 'Sorry, not being much help, are we? She grew up in Berkshire, I know that much. Winnersh rings a bell.'

'What about her parents?' said Munro. 'They'd have been devastated, would they not?'

'Oh, I'm sure of it, Inspector, if she'd had any. Her father died when she was young, in her teens, I think, and her mother a few years later. You can ask Harry about it when he comes back.'

'Aye, I will,' said Munro quietly. 'Thank you, I will. Well, we've taken up enough of your time already...'

'Nonsense,' said Ed. 'Pleasure to help.'

'Just one last thing before we go, are you absolutely sure there's no-one else your son might have called?'

'No, I don't think so,' said Ed, rubbing his chin. 'Can't think of... oh, Marcos! Dammit! How the heck could we forget about Marcos?'

'Of course!' said Clarissa. 'Marcos. How foolish of us, sorry Inspector, we'll be forgetting our own names next.'

'Quite alright,' said Munro, with an empathetic smile. 'I do it myself, sometimes. Cannae remember what I had for tea last night. So, who's this Marcos, then?'

'Marcos Alfonso Garcia Delgado. Mark, for short. Oh, I don't know how you'd describe him, they've known each other since forever.'

'Friends?'

'Well, yes, I suppose so,' said Clarissa, 'but they don't see each other very often. And they don't live that far apart, either. Different lifestyles, I suppose. He's a charming boy, though, simply delightful. An artist, don't you know? He's been here a few times. Gave Harry a lot of support when he was going through his drinking phase.'

'Yeah, stopped him falling over,' said Ed. 'Seriously, though, he wasn't like us, we were too soft on the kid. Marcos told it like it was, tore him to shreds about the booze. Did him good.'

'Would you have a telephone number? Or an address, perhaps.'

'No phone number, I'm afraid,' said Clarissa. 'But I think we've an address somewhere, I'll fetch it.'

* * *

West slumped in her seat, yawned and turned to face Munro as he reversed into the lane.

'What do you think?' she said.

'I think this case is like a tub of gravy granules.'

'What?'

'Thickens when you add water.'

'Very funny.'

'And you?'

'Well,' said West, 'I was thinking, the girl in that picture. His wife, Annabel. You know, if it wasn't for the long hair, I'd say she looked like a younger version of this Sheba character.'

'Right enough. Must be her double.'

'Well, obviously it's her double,' said West. 'Annabel's dead.'

'Is she?' said Munro.

'What do you mean?'

'You tell me, Charlie. You're a detective. For a start, there's no body.'

'I know,' said West, 'in case you weren't listening, she drowned, swept out to sea.'

'The tide was coming in.'

'Yes, but...'

'Look at the photo, Charlie.'

West pulled the frame from her bag and studied it carefully.

'What?'

'Look at her feet,' said Munro.

West drew a breath.

'Converse? Oh no, come on, not again, this was taken years ago!' she said, incredulously. 'Are you telling me she's still wearing...'

'You do a lot of walking, don't you, Charlie?' said Munro.

'What? Yes, of course I do,' said West.

'Like myself. You know, I get a new pair of boots every year; every year, and still I've not quite found the right ones. How are yours? Comfy, I imagine.'

'Are you kidding? I wouldn't wear them otherwise, would I? You should get some, I'm telling you, they're the best boots ever. God knows how many pairs I've been through, been wearing them for...'

Munro said nothing.

'Okay,' said West. 'Okay. Point taken.'

'There is no point,' said Munro. 'I'm just getting you to think, Charlie. The poor lassie's dead.'

'But she's just like the girl in those pics we found on his phone, surely that's too close to be a...?'

'Harry's type, that's all. We all have a type, Charlie. Even you.'

* * *

Sergeant Cole, enjoying the use of a desk and a private office – as opposed to the general mayhem on the ground floor – was happy to relinquish the tedious task of filling out charge sheets for something a little more investigative. Farnsworth-Brown's bank statements were conclusive evidence that, despite there being a healthy balance, the man was clearly not extravagant.

'Tommy,' said Munro as he and West ambled wearily through the door.

'Guv. Miss. I, er, borrowed your desk, miss, to go through... hope you don't...'

'No probs, Sergeant,' said West. 'Tell you what, I'll even stick the kettle on. How's that for role reversal?'

Munro shrugged his shoulders in response to Cole's look of bewilderment.

'How'd you get on, Tommy?' he said, grinning. 'Anything we should worry about?'

'Wouldn't say "worry", guv, but I'd say something's up.'

'What do you mean?'

'Well, looking at these, it's obvious he enjoyed his routine. See, on his current account, we've got the Co-Op, every Saturday, regular as clockwork. Then, there's the Chinese takeaway, once a week, every week. And every Monday, Wednesday and Friday, between two o'clock and ten past, £100 from the cash machine on the High Street. Then, suddenly, nothing. Not a single transaction, apart from a direct debit, that is.'

Munro slung his coat over the back of the chair and gently sat down.

'And he's not writing cheques?' he said. 'Not using another card?'

'Nope. He's got a MasterCard, but that's not been used in ages.'

'And the last transaction was…'

'Day before he went missing. Well, day before he was last seen, I should say. On the stairs.'

'I see,' said Munro, quietly, as he turned to face the window. 'I see.'

West glanced at Cole as an unexpected stillness descended on the room. Wary of breaking the silence, she carefully placed a mug of coffee on the desk and stared at Munro's baleful reflection. The furrowed brow. The hollow cheeks. The intense gaze. He looked, she thought, like a ghoul. Haunted.

'So,' she said softly, daring to shatter the peace, 'are you going to share it with us?'

Munro paused before speaking, his lips barely moving.

'This Harry fellow,' he said, as though talking to himself. 'He doesnae have any friends, so if he's gone away, he's gone alone. His folks don't think it odd, whereas his manager at the bar claims it's completely out of character and is, most certainly, a cause for concern. His car, like his flat and his phone, is as clean as a whistle. There's no trace of anything, not even a hair. And then there's this… this "Sheba". She confounds me. And why does she look strikingly similar to the lassie in the photo from the Farnsworth-Browns?'

'No,' he said, rising abruptly. 'No, no, something's not right here. I don't believe a fellow like this can just disappear. We've missed something. Get your coat. You too, Tommy.'

'Guv.'

'What?' said West. 'Where are we going?'

'Clock Court. His flat.'

71

'But… but it's getting late, can't it wait till…'

Munro glowered at West.

'Coming,' she said reluctantly.

* * *

West and Cole kept their distance as Munro, hands clasped firmly behind his back, trudged around the flat at a painstakingly slow pace, bending and stretching, scrutinising every book, every cupboard, every shelf, even the parquet flooring, for any signs of tampering; anything that may have been moved, intentionally or otherwise.

'So,' said West, with a huff, as she fiddled with her phone. 'What exactly are we looking for?'

'I'll tell you when we find it,' said Munro. 'And you can put that away.'

'But forensics have already been, they…'

'Forensics gave this place the once over, lassie, dabs and prints, that's all. They weren't looking for anything particular, anything specific. We are.'

'Like what, then?'

'As I said, I'll let you know.'

Munro reached the tiny, open plan kitchen and squinted as he scrupulously studied the wall which separated it from the living area. He tapped it with his knuckle, from top to bottom, from left to right. Hollow. He dropped to his knees and inspected the plinths beneath the units. There was a fine line of dirt between them and the floor. They had not been moved.

'We could be here for ages,' sighed West as they reached the bathroom. 'Do you really need all three of us to…'

'What do you think, Tommy?' said Munro, interrupting her. 'Of the bathroom?'

'Bit small, if you ask me, guv, considering the size of the place. I wouldn't be happy.'

'That's planners for you. No sense of proportion for the practicalities of life.'

'Fair size tub, though,' said Cole, 'I'll give 'em that. Jacuzzi too.'

'Aye. I'm sure Giuseppe would be proud.'

'Come again?'

'Giuseppe Jacuzzi. He invented it.'

'Really?' said Cole, impressed. 'Well, well, well, who'd have thought. I like the bath panel. Tongue and groove. Nice that. Can't beat real wood.'

Munro slowly shook his head.

'Tommy, Tommy, Tommy,' he said. 'I'm disappointed with you. It's MDF, can you not see that? Flashlight please.'

Munro fell gently to his knees and directed the beam around the edges of the panel, humming as he did so.

'I see,' he said, shining the torch at one corner. 'Ah-ha. Okay. Look here, the pair of you. Tell me, Charlie, what do you see?'

West stood beside Munro, leaned forward and did her best to look interested.

'Well,' she said. 'It's a bath panel. Wooden. White. And shiny, I mean glossy. Gloss paint.'

Munro sighed.

'Are you familiar with the saying "don't give up the day job?"' he said, softly.

'Yes.'

'Well, pay no heed, look at the screws, dammit! Can you not see that? The whole panel is in pristine condition apart from the screws, can you not see where the paint's come off? Someone's had this away. Tommy, have you a screwdriver? Pozi?'

Sergeant Cole unfurled a small driver from his Swiss Army knife, handed it over and waited silently as Munro methodically loosened all four screws and yanked the panel free.

'What the fuck?' said Cole, exasperated.

'Harry Farnsworth-Brown, I presume,' said Munro. 'Gloves please, Tommy. Charlie, you know the procedure, forensics and pathology, now. And I want uniform on the door, downstairs too.'

'Sir.'

Munro snapped on the latex gloves, crouched down on all fours and, one by one, dragged fourteen polythene sacks from beneath the tub.

'Nice of them to bag the evidence,' he said.

Sergeant Cole looked on, fascinated by the sight of the dismembered body parts, each individually sealed in airtight bags, feet, lower legs, thighs, upper arms, forearms, hands and head.

'It's like those barbecue portions you buy in the freezer place,' he said dryly.

Munro gazed curiously at a bag containing something resembling a pig's leg, minus the trotter, and prodded the anaemic flesh with his index finger.

'It'll be a Halal barbecue, Tommy,' he said.

'What? How'd you mean?' said Tommy.

'There's no juice. No blood.'

'No fingers.'

Tommy passed him a bag containing two hands. Two hands, two thumbs. No fingers.

'What do you think, guv? Triads? Yakuza? Get caught with his hands in the till?'

Munro smiled.

'No, no. I don't think so,' he said. 'But he'll not be playing the piano again, that's for sure. Charlie! Where are they?'

'On the way, sir,' said West as she hurried back. 'Couple of minutes.'

'Right. I want this place swept from top to bottom, every crack, every crevice. Leave no stone unturned, understand? And I want a positive ID on our friend here as soon as possible. We've got his head so it shouldn't be that...'

West froze at the sight of Farnsworth-Brown's serene-looking face behind the plastic, his flame-red hair trapped in the seal looking, to all intents and purposes, as though he'd suffocated. Her mouth filled with the bitter taste of bile, her stomach convulsed, and then she vomited into the wash basin.

'Dear, dear, dear,' said Munro. 'As if we haven't enough to clean up as it is.'

West wiped her mouth with a handful of toilet tissue.

'You've got your ID, sir,' she said, breathing heavily. 'That's him, alright. That's Harry Farnsworth-Brown. I recognise the head. Face. I mean face. Shit.'

* * *

Most of the diners were sipping cappuccinos, toying with their tiramisu, or indulging in liqueurs when Munro breezed in, walked straight to the rear of the restaurant and slumped, exhausted, in his usual booth. Piccolo was its usual, busy self. Alberto presented him with a small glass of Barolo.

'Is-a good to see you, James!' he said, beaming. 'And-a for you, tonight, especially, I have-a linguini with-a the seafood. Is-a beautiful!'

'No, thank you.'

'How about-a some chicken cacciatore? Very tasty, with-a garlic and-a rosemary.'

'No, thank you.'

'You wanna the steak, as usual?'

'Yes, please.'

'Burnt to a cinder, with-a roasted potatoes and-a the green beans?'

'Yes, please, Alberto.'

'No sauce?'

Munro shook his head, smiled politely, and tucked a napkin into his collar.

'Your-a mouth,' said Alberto, 'it must-a be so bored! One-a steak, coming up.'

A ravenous Munro coated his spuds with a generous sprinkling of salt and chomped on his charcoaled sirloin like a starving, stray cur, pausing only for the occasional sip of wine. 'Pardon', he muttered, as his cheeks puffed with a gratifying, silent belch. He pushed the empty plate to one side and contemplated a second glass of wine when a vivid image of Farnsworth-Brown, sprawled across the bed, flew into his mind. He grabbed his phone.

'Tommy? I hope I'm not disturbing you,' he said. 'Are you nearby?'

'Just having a pint, guv. Nightingale. What's up?'

'I'm not sure. Listen, will you meet me at the office, and I apologise now if I'm wasting your time.'

'No problem. Half an hour?'

'Thanks, Tommy, oh, and do you have that stick, with the photos on it?'

'It's in the safe.'

* * *

The office, save for the glow of the streetlights, was shrouded in darkness as they huddled over the laptop.

'Now, it's the ones of him on the bed, I want to see, Tommy,' said Munro. 'I want to see... there! That one, look, do you see that; by his leg?'

Cole squinted at the screen.

'Oh, yeah,' he said. 'Looks like a set of keys. I'll blow it up. Bit pixelated, but...'

'A Yale and a mortice...'

'Must've dropped them before he flaked out,' said Cole.

'No, no,' said Munro, standing up. 'Look, the fellow's come through the door, left his coat behind, then climbed the stairs to fall into his pit. He wouldnae carry his keys with him.'

'Fair point. So, what you're saying is...'

'Aye, those keys belong to whoever took the photo. And I'd wager that whoever took the photos, also bagged him into bite-sized portions.'

Cole leaned towards the screen as though it would improve the quality of the image.

'Funny fob,' he said. 'Looks like an earring.'

Munro stepped back and squinted at the blue and white disc on the screen.

'It's a Mati,' he said.

'A whati?'

'A Mati. It's a talisman, popular in Greece. Folk carry them, or hang them around the house. It's a kind of good luck charm – wards off the curse, the evil eye.'

'Could've used one of those when I got divorced,' said Cole. 'So, we're looking for Zorba the Greek, then?'

Munro smiled.

'No, someone superstitious, perhaps. Someone looking over their shoulder.'

* * *

D.S. West, dressing gown draped loosely around her shoulders, sat on the edge of the bed, opened the top drawer of the bedside cabinet and removed a small black suede box. She took the ring, slid it gently onto the third finger of her left hand and smiled ruefully as the stone glistened in the dim light. She sighed and turned to face the bearded barman slumbering in her bed. Her lip curled at the stench of his slimy hair gel, the juvenile tattoo proclaiming 'love' on the top of his arm, and the braided, leather bracelet wrapped around his wrist. He woke with a start as his jeans hit his face.

'Piss off,' she said, returning the ring to the drawer.

'What?'

'I've got work to do.'

'But it's… have you any idea what time it is?'

'You've got sixty seconds, or I'll call the police.'

'But you are the police,' he said, leaning back on his elbows, a cocky grin smeared across his face.

'Which is why you wouldn't want to meet my friends,' said West, fastening her gown and heading for the kitchen. 'They don't like it when one of their own is assaulted.'

'What? But I haven't…'

West stood in the doorway and held her wrists aloft.

'I've got the bruises,' she said. 'Clock's ticking.'

She cleared the table with a single sweep of the arm, showering the floor with half-eaten pieces of southern fried chicken and cold, greasy chips, opened her laptop and began trawling for Samantha Baker. It didn't take long to find her, or her address, or the fact that she was a fan of garage and hip-hop, margaritas and Keanu Reeves.

Annabel Parkes, however, was an altogether more private person. So private, in fact, that West could find nothing on her but old news items about the unfortunate incident in Aldeburgh, the newly-wed who drowned in the dead of night, the devastated husband, the coastguard search and the relentless efforts of the locals who'd spent days combing the beach for clues.

She scrolled through the list of others sharing the same name, those fortunate enough to still have a breath in their lungs – all fourteen of them. They were scattered across the country, from Hammersmith to Hertfordshire, Sunderland to Surrey, and Bangor to Berkshire. Berkshire. 'No,' she whispered incredulously, as another shot of vodka hit the back of her throat. 'Winnersh? Couldn't be.'

Munro did not take kindly to being woken at 4am.

'Meet me at the office,' he said tersely, 'eight o'clock sharp. And Charlie, don't be late.'

CHAPTER 9

"WHY DID YOU GET INVOLVED?"

Who knows? God knows. I don't know. Got carried away, I suppose. I was, intrigued. Captivated. Enthralled. She made it seem so... exciting. So interesting. It was like... it was like going on holiday for the first time, or learning a new skill. She'd have made a good teacher, her enthusiasm was contagious.

I had thought of getting out – splitting up, I mean – in the early days, when all she did was claw my back to shreds. I knew, even then, that there was something odd about her but she was like a magnet. Charismatic. I felt compelled to find out what was going on inside her head. You'd have thought, after the cigar box incident, that leaving would have been the easiest thing to do. It wasn't. It made it difficult. I knew it was wrong. Wrong. Sounds like an understatement. I thought, is she winding me up? Could she really have done it? I mean, really? Was she actually demented? Mad? Unstable? Or just a bit of a fruit loop? She wasn't on medication. She wasn't prone to wandering the streets at night, wringing her hands and mumbling gibberish to herself. What if I told the police and I was wrong? What then? I'd have looked a right fool and lost her as a friend. But what if I told the police and I was right? Could she cope with it all? The questioning? The interrogation? The psychoanalysis? The trial? The prison? The hatred? I'd lie awake at night, churning it over in my mind, not to mention my stomach. Worried. Confused. Scared, even. Then, next day, I'd see her again. And everything was back to normal. Everything was alright. I suppose, the thing is, when she talked about it, when she described what she'd done, it was as though she was somehow, detached, doing nothing more than relating a story. And that's how it affected me. I became detached. Like a farmer is with his cattle, or a doctor with his patients. Emotionally detached. It's the only way to deal with it.

Anyway, the day finally arrived when she popped the question. I half expected it, I think. She was in a playful mood, a bit hyper, frisky, and had managed to land a couple of champion bruises on my arms; not to mention a cut across my shoulder, all before dinner, after which I sat on the sofa and she, as usual, sat before me on the floor, cross-legged. First, there was the grin. Then, the tingle. 'Why don't we do one together?' she said. I nearly choked. 'It'll be fun,' she said. 'Another practice run.' A practice run? A practice run for what? 'What are you planning?' I asked, jokingly. 'A massacre?' She laughed and told me not to be so silly, she just had something a bit 'special' in mind. I had no idea what she was talking about but one thing was for sure, I wasn't going to be one half of a joint suicide pact. I agreed, kind of, just to keep her happy, for a couple of weeks at least, till she'd forgotten all about it. 'I'll think about it,' I said. 'I'll think about it.' Two days later, she said we were ready to roll.

She'd found him on the internet, on one of those local sites used for selling worthless tat that no-one in their right mind would buy if they were sober. A digital jumble sale. Then she did a bit of digging around, you know, Facebook, Twitter, that kind of thing, just to make sure he was suitable. Amazing what you can discover on the web. If a policeman asked you to surrender your details, you'd probably cry 'not without my lawyer', 'invasion of privacy', 'breach of human rights', but when it comes to the internet, people are, bizarrely, all too willing to expose themselves. This chap, who should have known better, was hiding his true identity behind the tag 'chantheman', which was about as effective as a false moustache and a pair of clear-glass spectacles. Real name: Jason Michael Chan. Born: Malaysia. Age: 28. Educated: APU, Kuala Lumpur. Status: Single. Parents: Two. Happily married and living in Toronto, Canada. Profession: Freelance Computer Geek. He would not, she said, be missed. Not for a while, at least.

We were going to buy a lawnmower. He had one, she didn't. 'We've come straight from work,' she said, justifying the rucksacks on our backs. As he wasn't expecting her to have company, she explained, much to his delight, that as a female of the species, she knew nothing of engines, whereas I, being a male, knew all there was to know about anything mechanical. 'No problem,' he said. 'We'll have a party.' It was obvious that 'chantheman' didn't get out much. He embraced our company like a ship-wrecked mariner who'd spent twenty years living off coconuts and raw fish in total isolation. His living room, workroom, workspace, call it what you will, looked like mission control at NASA. It was silent, bar the barely audible hum of a million computers linked to a million screens, each one displaying a different visual treat for the eyes; most of it, gobbledegook. I shudder to think how much technologically encrypted information was flying through the air and, more worryingly, through me.

Anyway, his initially nervous disposition soon turned to one of generosity as he plied us with drinks. Actually, he plied himself more than us. A couple of beers to start with, then he made himself a whisky mac. Then another. And another. And so it went on. He didn't actually tell us exactly what he did for a living, I mean, how he earned money. He could've been a spy for all I know, but he did take great delight in telling us what a genius he was. He pointed to a screen with a scrolling display of black and white characters and numerals. Royal Bank of Scotland. Apparently. Then, laptop in hand, he drew us to the window. We looked down at the street below, at a brand new, white Mitsubishi Shogun. It belonged to the family next door. He tapped the keyboard and grinned. The hazard lights came on. He tapped a few more keys, the engine started. He laughed out loud. 'Tapped into the car's wi-fi,' he said. 'Easy.' Impressive. To a degree. If you were in the market to be impressed. I wasn't. Computers are one thing. People are totally different. His social skills were lacking. He wasn't a good judge of character. He was too trusting.

I asked him about the lawnmower. He went into a bout of hysterical laughter. 'What would I be doing with a lawnmower?' he said. 'I'm on the first floor, I don't have a garden.' Touché. 'So, why are we here?' I asked. He said he was bored. Didn't like going out on his own. Thought he might meet some interesting people but, apart from us, every caller he'd had, had only been interested in the lawnmower. At that point, I was flummoxed. I didn't know where things were going. All I knew was, I'd read about people like Jason Michael Chan in the newspaper. For a fleeting moment, I actually thought it might be me who'd end up finely sliced in a bowl of black bean sauce. I didn't even know what she had in mind, it wasn't as though we had a plan and short of hitting him on the head with a frying pan, I could see no way of calming him down, let alone extinguishing him completely. Then the artist went to work. It was like watching a command performance. She grinned, a big, wide, friendly grin. 'Well, as we're having a party,' she said, 'we may as well have some fun.'

She stood up, took off her coat, slipped off her trainers and unbuttoned her shirt to the waist. His eyes nearly popped out of his head. She flirted with him outrageously, complaining about the heat, saying she felt hot. The more dishevelled she became, the higher his temperature rose, fuelled by the whisky macs she kept feeding him. I don't think the alcohol alone would've knocked him out, he was, undoubtedly, hardened to it, but he never noticed the powdered paracetamol she'd slipped into every glass. 64 tablets in all. It wasn't long before his liver sent out a distress signal and he collapsed on the floor. In a heap. Like a sack of bricks.

She giggled, mildly intoxicated, yet still managed to run through her 'procedure' with the efficiency of a paramedic attending an RTA. We donned our overalls, rolled him to one side of the room, spread out the groundsheet and rolled him back again. I was instructed to fetch whatever I could from the kitchen, saucepans or casseroles, if there wasn't a bucket, while she stripped him naked. By the time I'd returned, she'd already stabbed him with a needle and was ready to start syphoning off his blood. The casserole wasn't ideal, I lost count of the amount of trips I made to the sink and back, but eventually, there was nothing left.

'Are you sure he's dead?' I asked. 'He's twitching.'

'Spasms,' she said. 'It's like watching a dog dream, isn't it?'

She stroked his cheek with the back of her gloved hand, said it was a shame, that he was a nice chap. Friendly. Said he shouldn't be forgotten, that a souvenir was called for. Then she cut off his left ear, bagged it, and tossed it in her rucksack. After that, well, I felt like a spare part for the most, just watching from the sidelines. I mean, I have enough difficulty carving a chicken so it wasn't as though I could join in. She set about him with a scalpel, slicing and carving, sawing and pulling, grinning and giggling. She told me to pay attention. Next time, I'd have to do it myself. The head came off first, a swift cut from ear to ear; took a couple of goes because the blade's only so long but then, off it came. It looked like one of those dummies the hairdressers used to have in their windows to show off the latest styles. Then off came the hands, the feet and, well, the rest you know. All in all, it didn't take that long, really. We cleared everything away, put the groundsheet and his clothes in a bin sack for burning at the allotment, scrubbed the pans clean and bleached the sink. We sat with a scotch in hand staring at the pile of assorted appendages – the disassembled 'chantheman'.

She got up and walked around the flat, came back, sat down again and smiled. 'We've got a problem, Sweeney,' she said. She still had her sense of humour. 'Nowhere to put him.' She wasn't fazed, didn't fret, she was as calm as a mill pond. A mild panic caused my tummy to rumble. 'We can't carry him out,' I said. 'There's too much of him.' I leaned back against the sofa and looked skyward for divine intervention, although, with hindsight, I should have been looking in the other direction. Either way, our prayers were answered. There was a hatch in the ceiling. He had a loft. All we had to do was find a ladder. He kept it in the bedroom, behind the door. I didn't venture all the way in, no need, besides, it was too dark. I fumbled around, cautiously, lest I disturb a false widow spider or a roof rat, and that's where 'chantheman' went. His days of luring unsuspecting visitors to his flat under false pretences were over.

CHAPTER 10

SPRATT HALL ROAD, WANSTEAD. 5:50am
Munro stopped dead in his tracks. There was little that
shocked him, but the sight of D.S. West sitting at her desk,
knocked him for a six.

'Do you know what time it is?' he said, flabbergasted.

West glanced at the wall clock.

'Early,' she said, matter of factly.

The glare of the laptop accentuated the bags under her
eyes. Her face creased with a smile.

'I've been busy,' she said. 'Up all night. Tea?'

'Aye,' said Munro as he placed a greasy, paper bag on
his desk and removed his coat. 'That would be most
welcome. Have you had yourself some breakfast?'

West hesitated.

'Yes, thanks,' she said. 'I had some... some muesli.
Before I left. Muesli and yogurt.'

Munro said nothing, simply shook his head, opened the
bag and handed her one half of a toasted, bacon sandwich.

'So,' he said. 'What have you got?'

'Samantha Louise Baker,' said West, devouring the
sarnie. 'The ex. She's living in Waterloo.'

'Waterloo?' said Munro. 'Is that not a wee bit metropolitan, for someone of her breeding? Mind you, I suppose she could be living in one of those fancy riverside apartments.'

''Fraid not,' said West. 'Ospringe House, Wootton Street. It's a council flat. Couldn't find anything about her on the work front, though.'

'And you're sure it's her?'

''Positive. Her Facebook page is so old it even has a few pics of Harry on it.'

'Is that so? Good work, Charlie. I'm impressed. We'll pay her a visit, right enough. Is that it?'

'Not quite,' said West. 'You'll like this. Annabel Parkes. You were right.'

'I was? That's nice to know,' said Munro. 'In what way, exactly?'

'She's not dead.'

Munro stopped chewing.

'Sorry, Charlie,' he said, ''tis early yet and I've not finished my breakfast. Say that again.'

'Annabel Parkes. She didn't drown.'

'What?'

'She's alive and well. And living in Winnersh.'

Munro chuckled to himself.

'Och, no, you must be wrong, lassie. That theory was intended as an exercise to make you think, that's all. Must be another Annabel Parkes. Must be hundreds of them.'

'There are,' said West. 'But only one in Winnersh.'

Munro eased himself into his chair, crossed his legs and regarded West curiously.

'Come on then, Charlie,' he said. 'Enlighten me. If she's not dead, what do you think happened?'

'I'm thinking that she faked her own death.'

'I see. And why would that be?'

'Who knows? Fed up? Not cut out for marriage? Someone else on the side?'

Munro dusted the crumbs from his fingertips and reached for his tea.

'All the obvious reasons. No. Sorry, Charlie. I don't buy it. Do you not think they'd have checked her out when she went missing? They would have...'

'They didn't,' said West, abruptly. 'I've been through the records. The inquiry focused on Aldeburgh and the search and rescue. They didn't bother looking any further.'

'Didn't try her home address? Didn't inform the parents?'

'What parents? You know she didn't have any, the Farnsworth-Browns told us as much.'

'I still don't buy it. You're telling me a girl disappears, presumed drowned, then pops up...'

'With all due respect, sir,' said West, raising her voice. 'She's the only Annabel Parkes, with an 'e', living in Winnersh, and has done for years, she's still on the electoral register, it's just too much of a...'

'Okay,' said Munro, sighing as he tossed the crumpled bag to the bin. 'Okay. I give in. We'll make her our second port of call.'

* * *

From behind the rain-spattered windscreen, Ospringe House looked as cold and foreboding as a Dickensian workhouse, the doorways draped in shadows of gloom and despair. An anonymous looking male, dressed in jogging pants and a hoodie, emerged from one of the flats on the ground floor, followed by a tan and white Staffie wearing a collar resembling a medieval instrument of torture.

'Let's hope that's not her husband,' said Munro.

Samantha Baker did not, thought West, resemble a typical council house tenant. She eyed the black, two-piece suit, the court shoes and the remarkably flawless skin – which would have been more at home in the City or the wine bars of Maida Vale – with more than a hint of jealousy.

'Miss Baker?' she said sternly, holding up her warrant card.

'Yes. What's the matter?'

'Detective Sergeant West, this is D.I. Munro. Mind if we ask you a few questions? It's about a Mr Farnsworth-Brown.'

'Farns... you mean Harry? Whatever's...'

'May we come in?'

The flat, observed Munro, belied its grim exterior, a far cry from the schemes north of the border. With its Farrow & Ball paintwork and White Company furnishings, it resembled a feature from the pages of *Homes & Garden*. He glanced around the lounge, a look of mild bewilderment on his face.

'Not what you expected?' said Baker.

'No,' said Munro, smiling. 'It is not. And that's a compliment, mind.'

'Thank you. So, what's old Harry been up to then? Haven't seen the bugger since... yonks. Haven't seen him in yonks.'

'I'm afraid,' said West, with a sycophantic tilt of the head, 'I'm afraid he's passed away.'

'What? But... but that's ridiculous!' said Baker, eyes wide in disbelief. 'He can't have, he was fine, we only... I mean, he's so young. Bloody hell. Bloody hell, what was it? Heart attack? A car accident?'

'Something like that,' said Munro. 'I'm afraid we can't say too much at this stage, you understand?'

Baker sat down, stood up, lit a cigarette, and sat down again.

'Of course,' she said, drawing hard. 'Shit. Sorry, it's a bit of a shock, that's all.'

'I understand,' said Munro. 'It's not a pleasant experience, being told...'

'Not like this, not out of the blue, just when you least expect it. No warning. If he'd been ill... Shit. Shit.'

Munro gave her a moment to collect her thoughts before continuing.

'You and Harry,' he said. 'How did you meet? Would it have been at university, perhaps?'

'What? Oh, yes, sorry. Yes.'

'And you had a relationship?'

'A relationship?' said Baker. 'What's that got to do with anything? Why are you asking me about...?'

'Just curious,' said Munro calmly. 'No need to get upset. Sometimes folk remember things; things which might help. So, you had a relationship?'

'No. Yes, yes, we did. If you can call it that, more of a... it didn't last long, he enjoyed his books too much, not like me. But it was fun. While it lasted.'

'Not like you?' said Munro.

'No. Harry was very studious, I was into the fun aspect of student life, Inspector. I'm what you might call, "a people person".'

'So, you didn't graduate then?' said West, cynically.

Baker sat back and eyed West with a look of contempt.

'Au contraire, Sergeant...'

'Detective Sergeant,' said West.

'I graduated with honours. First Class. Politics. Don't suppose many police officers can say that, can they?'

Munro smiled at the smouldering catfight.

'Politics?' he said.

'Yes, I was going to change the world, Inspector, then...'

'Then?'

'Life. Too much alcohol, too many Es, an STD and a nervous breakdown.'

West shuffled nervously on her feet as she recognised her traits.

'Still, things can't be that bad,' she said. 'I mean, look around you, it must have cost a fair bit to kit this place out.'

'Bank of mum and dad. They refuse to see me – that's what you get for throwing your life away – but they won't let me starve.'

'If we could get back to Harry, Miss Baker,' said Munro. 'Would I be right in thinking the last time you saw him was in Aldeburgh? At the festival?'

'Aldeburgh?' said Baker. 'No, that was... oh, the festival? Christ, that's going back a bit but, yes, yes, come to think of it, I suppose it was. That's right, I remember now, it was quite funny really, he had one hell of a terrier with him.'

'A terrier?'

'His latest squeeze. Had him by the ankles. She was really quite frightening, went ballistic when she saw us together, ranted on at him for ages.'

'Do you know why?' said West.

'No idea. I was off my head, so I didn't care, really. She came across as quite possessive.'

'I see,' said Munro. 'And this possessive lass, the terrier, that would be Annabel Parkes, would it not?'

'Annabel? Don't be silly, what's she got to do with it?'

'Sorry,' said Munro, surprised. 'We must be at cross purposes here. You see, you say you remember Harry with a girl at the festival.'

'That's right.'

'And so far as we know, the girl with Harry, was Annabel Parkes.'

West shot Munro a furtive glance as she rifled through her bag and produced the small, framed photograph from the Farnsworth-Browns.

'Here,' she said, passing it to Baker. 'This is Harry and Annabel.'

Baker frowned as she stared at the photo and shook her head.

'I don't know where you got this from,' she said. 'But that's not Annabel.'

'What?'

'It's not Annabel, I should know, we hung out together, pubs mainly, or the student bar. She was studying medicine, I think, or biology, something to do with bodies, anyway. She was tall and lean, five-ten at least, skinny as a rake with jet black hair.'

'So, you've no idea who this girl is?' said Munro.

'Sorry. Although…'

'Go on.'

'No, it's silly,' said Baker. 'I just thought, she does look a bit like the girl he was with in Aldeburgh.'

'Really? Are you sure about that?'

'No. Couldn't swear to it. It was long time ago and, like I said, I was plastered.'

'Not to worry. And you've not seen Harry since?'

'You're kidding, aren't you? Why would I want to see Harry? We had a fling. That was it.'

'So, you've not bumped into each other? Met for a coffee, maybe?' said Munro.

'Don't be absurd, Inspector,' said Baker, donning her cap and coat. 'I've moved on, we both have. Now, if you don't mind, I'm going to be late if I don't get a scoot on.'

* * *

'Well, well, well,' said Munro as he fastened his seat belt. 'The gravy thickens.'

West sat staring into space as the rain peppered the roof of the car.

'What do you mean?' she said quietly.

Munro sighed, deflated at her lack of perception.

'Call Tommy,' he said. 'Give him Baker's description and tell him he's to go to Clock Court and wait. See if she shows up. Which she will.'

'What?' said West. 'You've lost me, why would Baker be going to…'

'Because she's lying. She was still seeing Harry after he and Annabel were married, and I've a hunch she saw him recently, a few days ago, maybe.'

'That's ridiculous, how can you be so…'

'Instinct, Charlie. Instinct.'

'Instinct?'

'And the way she reacted when you mentioned Harry's passing. That's not the way folk react to news of a death when they haven't seen the person for a few years.'

'Some people can't handle grief,' said West.

'What was she wearing, Charlie?' said Munro. 'Just now, when she left?'

'Er, cardigan. And a hat. Woolly hat.'

'Ring any bells?'

West threw her head back and groaned in frustration.

'Of course, the girl on the stairs. Christ, I'm… what now?'

'Winnersh,' said Munro. 'Quick as we can. Lights and music, please Charlie, no time to lose.'

* * *

Woodward Close was the antithesis of Sammy Baker's bleak urban retreat. A quiet, tree-lined cul-de-sac, speckled with overbearing, mock-Tudor new-builds, immaculate front lawns and driveways crammed with top of the range saloons used for the exclusive purpose of ferrying fodder from the supermarket on Sunday afternoons.

'Nice here,' said West. 'It's so quiet. So green.'

'It's God's waiting room,' said Munro, grimacing. 'Move here and you'll die a premature death.'

The bell resounded with a tinny rendition of Big Ben building up to the hourly chime, which Munro impatiently interrupted with a couple of hefty raps on the brass knocker.

'Bet you hate queuing, don't you?' said West with a smirk.

'I hate everything, Charlie.'

A prim lady, late sixties, wearing gardening gloves and clutching a pair of secateurs, opened the door with a brisk yank.

'Dead-heading,' she said, with all the assertiveness of a schoolmistress. 'Takes an age to come through from the garden. Police officers?'

'What?' said West. 'I... yes, but how did you...'

'Come, come, dear, don't you watch television? You all look the bloody same. How can I help?'

Munro proffered his card.

'D.I. Munro,' he said, with an endearing wink, 'and this here, is Detective Sergeant Charlotte West. I'm afraid we may have disturbed you quite unnecessarily, though. You see, we were looking for Annabel Parkes.'

'You've found her. What of it?'

'This appears to be an unholy coincidence,' said Munro apologetically. 'We were looking for someone, how can I put this, a wee bit younger.'

'You'll be after my daughter, then. Bella. Same name, half the genes. You'd better come in before the neighbours start twitching.'

The lounge, clearly reserved for the purposes of entertaining, was a dust-free environment furnished with an eclectic mix of bric-a-brac, a floral print, three-piece suite and the heady scent of a lavender pot-pourri.

'Do sit down,' said Mrs Parkes. 'You're making the place look untidy. Can I get you something? Tea, coffee, something a little stronger, perhaps. I know you chaps are fond of a tipple, isn't that right? I've got some cherry brandy somewhere.'

'Thank you, no, madam,' said Munro, grinning widely, 'we'll not keep you long.'

'Very well. Come on then, what's all this about Annabel? What's the silly mare been up to, now?'

'Nothing,' said West. 'At least, nothing we know of. We're trying to corroborate somebody else's... we're looking for someone.'

'I see,' said Mrs Parkes. 'How terribly dull.'

'Before we go any further,' said Munro. 'I wonder if you'd mind taking a look at this picture for us.'

'Do you recognise the girl?' said West, passing her the framed photo.

''Fraid not.'

'So, that's not your daughter?'

'More's the pity, looks a darn site healthier,' said Mrs Parkes.

'How about the gentleman?'

'Sorry. They do make a fine couple, though. What's happened? Have they gone missing? Eloped, perhaps?'

'That's what we're trying to find out,' said Munro. 'Could I trouble you for a photo of your daughter? Just to look at, mind.'

'There, on the sideboard,' said Mrs Parkes. 'It's the only one I keep out, she looked so fresh, then.'

'Then?' said West. 'Did she change?'

'She became jaded. Oh, she was still the tallest, scrawniest bag of bones ever to wander the streets of Winnersh, but her spark had gone, she looked so gaunt. That hair didn't help either, she looked as if she was off to a Halloween party.'

'Any idea why?' said West. 'Was she stressed? Pressure of exams?'

Mrs Parkes threw her head back and laughed.

'Stress?' she said. 'Bella was too spaced out to get stressed, dear. Too much weed, nothing serious, but enough to distract her.'

'I see,' said Munro. 'Tell me, would you happen to know if she was friends with a lassie by the name of Baker? Samantha Baker?'

'Couldn't tell you, Inspector. We didn't speak then and she hardly keeps in touch now, bar the occasional email or a card on my birthday. What of it?'

'Oh, a similar tale from one of her university friends, that's all,' said Munro. 'Do you think we might have a word with Annabel?'

'You'll have to shout, Inspector. She's in Perth.'

Munro's face broke into a wide-eyed smile.

94

'Perth!' he said, beaming. 'My, my, I've many a memory of Perth, tis a braw place, that's for sure.'

'Really?'

'Oh, aye, the view from Ben Lawers across the loch, the sun glinting off the water, the gorge at Killiecrankie; come on, ye Jacobites!'

Mrs Parkes, arms folded, regarded Munro with an air of bemusement.

'Australia,' she said. 'Perth. Australia.'

'Oh. When, er, when did she go?'

'Four years ago, Inspector. Four years.'

'And she's not been back? At all? Ever?' said Munro.

'She prefers eating barbecued prawns in the company of convicts these days, Inspector. Can't imagine why she'd want to come back, anyway, she doesn't know anyone here, anymore. The only friends she ever made had eight legs and crawled around decaying wood stumps. Even then, she took great pleasure in slicing them any which way she could.'

'I'm sorry?' said West.

'Entomologist, dear. That's what she wanted to be, and that's what she is now, only in Perth, where I imagine her specimens are a great deal larger than those she'd find here. Murdoch University, that's where you'll find her, should you fancy the trip.'

* * *

Munro, head bowed, ambled pensively down the garden path as the front door closed behind them. He paused by the car, looked at West and stared right through her as she fumbled with her phone.

'Missed call,' she said. 'Sergeant Cole. Shall I call him back?'

Munro was miles away.

'Who's the girl in the photo, Charlie?' he said, rhetorically. 'Who the hell was Harry married to?'

* * *

95

'Tommy,' said Munro as they stomped through the door.

'Guv. Miss. How was Berkshire?'

'Leafy,' said Munro. 'Like a morgue in autumn.'

'I liked it,' said West. 'Might move there one day.'

'Let me know. I'll send you a wreath.'

Sergeant Cole smiled and filled the kettle.

'That woman you asked me to look out for, guv,' he said. 'Short, funny hat, cardigan, she showed up about an hour and a quarter after you called.'

Munro glanced at West and winked.

'And then?'

'Not much,' said Cole. 'Funny thing was, she looked like she knew where she was going, had quite a pace on, then stopped dead when she caught sight of uniform on the main door. Hovered for a bit, then turned turtle and scarpered.'

'Thanks, Tommy,' said Munro with a knowing smile. 'Charlie, make a note, Samantha Baker. Tomorrow morning. Anything else?'

'Couple of things. Lab report on your desk, guv,' he said. 'Results on Farnsworth-Brown.'

Munro sat back, rubbed his eyes and opened the envelope.

'Just as I thought,' said Munro. 'The wee man's as dry as a bone, and he's that well preserved, they cannae give a time of death.'

'Says a lot for freezer bags,' said West. 'Speaking of food…'

'Charlie,' said Munro. 'The name of that fella, the one who knew Harry? Mark…'

'Marcos Delgado?'

'Aye, that's the chap. Give him a call, we need a chat, soon as.'

'Okay,' said West. 'I'll just grab us a bite to eat first, what would you…'

'Call first, please, Charlie; won't take long. And if there's no answer, find an address, can't be that many Delgados about the place.'

Sergeant Cole placed a mug of tea on Munro's desk and hovered uncomfortably.

'What is it, Tommy? You've your doorstep face on.'

'You're familiar with the phrase "it never rains", aren't you, guv?'

'Indeed.'

'Well, it's pissing down.'

'Come again?'

'We've got another,' said Cole. 'Body, that is.'

'Are you joking me?'

'Nope.'

'Where?' said Munro.

'Herongate Road.'

'Herongate? Dear, dear. Probably some poor, wee pensioner who cannae afford to heat the house or...'

'Close,' said Cole. 'They found him in the attic.'

'The attic? Now, why on earth would he be sleeping in the...'

'In pieces. Like Farnsworth-Brown. Only, he wasn't bagged up.'

'Oh. I see.'

'D.S. Ashford from Chingford's down there now.'

'Right, I'm away,' said Munro. 'Charlie, have you an address for our Spanish friend?'

'Yes, I think so, but...'

'Get a number for young Annabel Parkes, too, while you're at it. In Australia. Call her mother if you have to. I'll not be long.'

'But what about lunch?'

'You should have had some fruit with your muesli.'

CHAPTER 11

"WHY DID SHE DO IT?"

Good question, but you're asking the wrong person. You probably want me to say it was because she was unbalanced, unhinged, deranged, demented. Not the full shilling. But I won't. Because she wasn't. A bit of OCD and an inquiring mind, yes, but you can't hang her for that.

Look, it's like those people who swim the channel or climb Mont Blanc or run 100 metres in a straight line. They're not mad, are they? So, why do they do it? To get to France? To reach the summit? To break the tape? No. Of course not. They do it so they can attain a sense of achievement. A feeling of self-worth. I think it's because they harbour some kind of insecurity. There's something in their make-up, something in their past, that compels them to prove to themselves, and the world, that they are the best. She had nothing to prove. She was just an unqualified pathologist without a position who had to find her own bodies. She had a passion for it, she was good at it, and she liked to practice whenever she could. And she must have practiced a lot, believe me. I can't say for certain how many she'd done, I mean, I only know about the chap in the plastic bags and 'chantheman', of course, but she must have done a few, stands to reason, you don't acquire skills like that overnight. It was like watching a master butcher at work, the way she jointed the body, every cut was clean, no ragged edges, no torn sinews, no broken bones. Her hand was steady, her approach methodical; her concentration unwavering. No breaks, no pauses, no fear, not even a drop of sweat. And she was fast. Deftly fast.

I think part of the attraction was the fact that she didn't... I mean, she wasn't like the stereotyped image of a crackpot. She didn't stare vacuously into space and she wasn't simmering waist-deep in a cauldron of hate, bubbling with anger, a chip on each shoulder. There was no malice in what she did. There was no axe to grind. She didn't despise her victims. Quite the contrary. She liked them. She befriended them to assess their suitability. She said their mental and emotional disposition would determine whether they'd be viable candidates for the op or if they were to be consigned to the 'not suitable' list. Maybe it had something to do with samsara. Perhaps that was it, perhaps she figured the ones she chose had a better-than-evens chance of reaching enlightenment.

Okay, I know what you're thinking. You're thinking that if she wasn't completely barking, then she must have got some kind of perverse, twisted kick out of it. Maybe she was some kind of closet feminist who got turned on by carving up men. But no. She wasn't. And no, she didn't. I admit, the 'idea' of doing it excited her and simply talking about it made her... frisky, but the actual act, the actual process of extinguishing a life and transforming the body into take-away-sized portions, well, that was clearly a brilliant, and almost scientific exercise in dismemberment.

Even as a kid, when she wasn't culling the insect population of her back garden, she'd turn her attention to anything she could lay her hands on, just to find out what went where, and why, and how. Like a toaster, taken apart, its component parts laid out on the table. As individual items, they meant nothing, but as a part of something bigger, they suddenly became integral to the functioning form. Just as an automatic kettle is useless without a thermostat, so a body is useless without a brain.

Or maybe I've got it all wrong. Maybe it's more deep-rooted than that. Maybe she suffered from the unquantifiable consequences of bereavement. Death. The loss of her father at such a young age. That's a cliché for the couch if ever there was one, only problem with that theory is that she didn't hate life, nor did she resent being alive. She relished it.

So, I'm afraid I can't tell you why she did it, all I know is, you can read too much into it. You can go over the suppositions, the whys and wherefores, until you're blue in the face. You can blame it on her childhood or the parents or even a gene mutation but the bottom line is, she simply upgraded from pulling legs off spiders to dissecting her own species.

CHAPTER 12

FLAT B, HERONGATE ROAD, WANSTEAD. 3:12pm
The house was typical of the area: a large, run-of-the-mill,
Victorian terrace comprising two floors, each hastily
converted into one-bedroom flats with scant regard for
planning permission or the safety of its occupants. A lone
WPC stood guard by the front door as a line of blue and
white tape, strung around the block-paved drive, flapped
and rustled in the wind. Munro said nothing, flashed his
warrant card, and smiled politely.

'Upstairs, sir,' said the WPC. 'Top floor.'

D.S. Jeff Ashford, a crinkly, forty-something with a
face weathered by nicotine and a belly swollen by London
Pride, met Munro at the top of the stairs and sighed.

'James,' he said, mournfully, as he ruffled his mop of
auburn hair. 'How's it going?'

'Same as, Jeff. Same as. And yourself?'

'The usual. Over-worked and underpaid. Don't know
how you do it.'

'Do what, exactly?'

'Keep going.'

'Porage,' said Munro, with a wry grin. 'Just water and
salt, mind. No milk.'

'Somehow, I think retirement will taste better.'

'So, what have we got?'

'Enough to make you glad you didn't have a full English.'

'That bad?'

'Worse,' said Ashford. 'People downstairs got pissed off at the noise going on all night, some sort of alarm, they said. They knocked the door and weren't too keen on the smell either, so they gave us a bell, or rather, Tommy. About seven, it was. They were adamant the bloke was in so we gave the door a nudge.'

'And?'

'And... the "alarm" was a computer, one of his computers, making a heck of a racket it was, all pinging and whirring. And there were flies like bluebottles, clambering at the window. We had a nose around and that's when we found him. Them. His bits. All chopped up. In the loft.'

Ashford buttoned his once fashionable jacket at the waist, handed Munro a pair of gloves, and led him into the flat. Two Scenes of Crimes Officers, wearing face masks and body suits, were finishing up, systematically bagging anything they could lay their hands on – from external disks and flash drives, to an empty bottle of scotch – while a skinny young man with a shaved head and a tattoo on his neck, tapped furiously at a keyboard.

'This is Sean,' said Ashford. 'His bark's worse than his bite.'

Sean stopped typing, turned, and smiled at Munro.

'Inspector,' he said, with a cut-glass accent. 'How are you?'

'Relieved,' said Munro, grinning. 'Are you here on work experience? You look awfully young.'

'I'm 26, Inspector. Been doing this for years.'

'26? My, my, not long till you get the gold watch, then. I take it you know your way round this pile of... technology?'

'Could do it blindfolded,' said Sean. 'From the other room.'

'Ah, the arrogance of youth, eh, Jeff. So, don't keep us in suspense, laddie, what have you found? Can you tell us who he is?'

'I can do better than that, Inspector,' said Sean. 'I could probably tell you everything about him.'

'I'm listening,' said Munro.

'Okay. Name's Jason Chan. Malaysian. Age, 34. He's been here eight years, bit of a whizz on the techno front, not in our league, but good enough. From what I can gather, he was into building algorithms, writing scripts and codes. Back-end stuff. And for kicks, he seemed to enjoy hacking. He dabbled with Anonymous and was personally responsible for taking down more than a few corporate websites, blue-chip companies, that kind of thing.'

'I see. And apart from the obvious, the hacking,' said Munro, 'you think he's legit?'

'Seems to be,' said Sean. 'He's got a bunch of regular clients by the looks of it, and the only people outside of them he's been in regular contact with are his parents. Canada. Aside from that, I've got pretty much everything you need to know about him: bank details, tax code, National Insurance number, hobbies, where he shopped, in fact, his life story if you want it.'

'Excellent,' said Munro, pondering his next question. 'You say he's Malaysian?'

'That's right. Born Shah Alam, educated Kuala Lumpur.'

Munro looked at Ashford and frowned.

'It's probably nothing,' he said, 'but if he's Malaysian, he'd be a Muslim, would he not?'

'Don't ask me,' said Ashford, with a shrug of the shoulders. 'Haven't a clue.'

'He might be,' said Sean. 'Coming from Shah Alam, but then again, there's every chance he could be a Hindu, or a Buddhist, even.'

'I suppose, what I mean is, Sean, you've not found anything, untoward?' said Munro. 'Anything vaguely suspicious?'

'No, sir.'

'Okay. Good. Jeff, a wee favour, if you will. I know it's not your patch, but once we're done here, can you chase the DNA profile for me, so we can get a formal ID, please,'

'No probs,' said Ashford.

'Then send it over to CT Command, make sure he's not on their list of suspects. I'd hate to think we'd had a terrorist in our midst and no-one spotted him.'

Ashford nodded.

'So, how about a time of death?' said Munro. 'Have we a clue about that?'

'Initial estimate, they reckon within the last 48 hours, 36 maybe.'

Sean spun around in his chair.

'I can tell you who did it, if you like,' he said, cockily. 'Well, probably, did it.'

Munro glanced at Ashford then slowly turned to face Sean. His eyes narrowed as he bit his bottom lip.

'Say that again,' he said, his voice barely more than a whisper.

'I think I know who did it,' said Sean. 'Not that I'm a detective or anything, but look, here, I've pulled up all his emails and texts. He was selling a lawnmower…'

'What? Are you joking me?' said Munro with a huff. 'Why on earth would he… was he mowing the carpet?'

'No idea,' said Sean. 'Point is, he was selling it. Had it on this "pre-loved" sort of website, you know, like a local eBay, called himself "chantheman".'

'Sounds like a dope dealer.'

'Here's the thing, someone came to see it, that is, they arranged to see it, night before last. I'm guessing they showed up. Meeting tallies with the time of death.'

Munro turned to Ashford.

'Jeff. Neighbours. Any sightings of anyone coming or going?'

'Nothing.'

'Okay. Well, let's assume, for now, they slipped in unnoticed. Go on, Sean, what else?'

'Here's the correspondence between him and the buyer, someone called Sheba.'

Munro let out a short, blunt gasp, as though he'd been thumped on the back. He looked at Sean, a startled expression on his face.

'Have I hit a nerve?' said Sean.

'I think you may have severed it, laddie. Sheba, you say? And you're sure of it?'

'Positive. It's all here.'

'Okay, listen, Sean, this is very important, do you have the email address?'

'Had. It was active for three days, then deleted. Hotmail. Sheba745.'

'Damn and blast, and there's no way of...'

'Not a Hotmail address, no. Same as Yahoo. Free. No questions asked. Besides, you can put in any info you want when you sign up, doesn't have to be factual.'

'Mother of... and there's no trace of any calls?' said Munro, scratching the back of his head. 'No text messages confirming the meeting or...'

''Fraid not. Just the emails. Sorry.'

Munro, scowling with frustration, slowly turned on his heels and scanned the room, from the door to the desk to the open hatch to the loft, before moving to the kitchen. His nose twitched, irritated.

'Jeff,' he said. 'Here, a moment. Can you smell that?'

Ashford joined him, tilted his head back and sniffed the air.

'Nope. What are we sniffing for?'

'Bleach. There's the scent of bleach in the air. It's down the sink. Get someone under there, look in the trap, and check the drains outside. Something's been flushed down there, I'd like to know what.'

Ashford sighed.

'If you say so, James,' he said. 'But I reckon you're wasting your time; people chuck bleach down the plughole all the time.'

Munro smirked and regarded Ashford with tilt of the head.

'Look around you, Jeff,' he said softly. 'What do you see?'

'Well, nothing. It's spotless.'

'Does that not strike you as odd?'

'Odd? No, why…'

'Look through there, where he worked, what's it like?'

'Like my son's bedroom, a tip.'

'So why is it so clean in here, especially if he had company? No cups, no glasses, even the bin's empty.'

'Well, I suppose he could have been…'

'He could have been a lot of things, but house-proud, he was not. What about prints? Have we anything obvious yet? If he had visitors, surely there must be something…'

'We'll know for sure by the morning,' said Ashford, 'but so far, it looks as though he was on his lonesome.'

'No,' said Munro, staring at the sink. 'He wasn't. Of that, I'm sure.'

* * *

D.S. West rammed the remnants of a chocolate digestive into her mouth, scattering crumbs across her desk as Munro flew through the door.

'Did you find your pensioner?' she mumbled, holding up an empty mug. 'What was it? Cardiac?'

'Not a pensioner, Charlie. Another Harry.'

'What?'

'Hacked to pieces. Name of Jason Chan. Aye, tea please. Tommy, first thing tomorrow, call Jeff at

106

Chingford, see if they've the DNA profile back, will you? Oh, and prints, too.'

'Guv.'

'Charlie. Annabel Parkes. Number, please.'

'You seem flustered,' said West, handing him a mug.

'Not flustered, Charlie. It's what we call "adopting a sense of urgency". Two bodies, one square mile. We have to move on this. Incidentally, this Jason Chan, have a guess at who the last person was to see him alive?'

'No idea,' said West. 'Surprise me.'

'Sheba.'

'You're…'

'I kid you not. What's the time?'

'Five. Give or take.'

'That makes it 1am in Perth,' said Munro. 'Let's give her a wee call.'

'At this hour?' said West. 'She'll be in bed, surely?'

'Nae bother. She'll have to get up to answer the phone anyway. That picture of Harry and the lassie, copy it onto your phone, quick now, we'll need to send it to her.'

Munro, spectacles perched on the end of his nose, took a slug of tea, read the piece of paper at arm's length and carefully dialled the number, clearing his throat as it rang through.

'Annabel. What's up?' came the voice at the other end.

'Miss Parkes?'

'That's right. Who is this?'

'You won't know me. My name's Munro. Detective Inspector James Munro. I'm calling from Wanstead C.I.D., in London.'

'Police? Christ! What's happened? Is it mum?'

'No, no, she's fine. Just fine,' said Munro. 'Now, you'll not thank me for calling at this hour, I'm sure, but I wonder, might we have a wee chat? It won't take long.'

'I guess so,' said Parkes.

'Excellent, I'll be as quick as I can. We're trying to trace a missing person; someone you may have known. Chap by the name of Farnsworth-Brown, Harry Farnsworth-Brown.'

'Never heard of him.'

'You're sure?'

'Think I'd remember a name like that,' said Parkes. 'What makes you think I'd know him?'

'He was courting, I mean, seeing, a friend of yours. Samantha Baker?'

'Samantha? That's going back a bit. Oh, it's not her, is it? Nothing's…'

'No, no. She's fine, too,' said Munro. 'Nothing to worry about, there. She's living in London. Waterloo, actually. Back to this Farnsworth-Brown chappie, we need to find him, and a young girl he was seen with. I've a photo of them, as a couple, would you mind if I sent it to you, on the email? You might…'

'Email? How did you get my…'

'I'm a detective, Miss Parkes.'

'Fair enough,' she said, laughing politely down the phone. 'Do you want to send it now?'

Munro nodded at West.

'Thanks, you should have it in a moment or two. Chances are you probably won't…'

'Christ almighty,' said Parkes, as she opened the image. 'Where did you get this?'

Munro snatched his glasses from his face and sat bolt upright.

'What is it?' he said. 'Do you recognise him?'

'No, don't know him from Adam, but she…'

'She?'

'She's trouble,' said Parkes. 'If she's gone missing, hopefully it's off the edge of a cliff.'

'You know her?' said Munro.

'Kind of.'

'Listen, if there's anything you can tell us about her, anything at all…'

'She used to hang around the campus…'

'She was a student?'

'No, she flunked,' said Parkes. 'Didn't have the grades to get in, but she virtually lived there. At first I thought, good for her, she was obviously dedicated, wanted to learn, spent all her time in the library.'

'And no-one thought to remove her? If she wasn't a student...'

'Everyone turned a blind eye, especially the staff, she could charm the pants off a priest. Obviously, she didn't, couldn't, attend lectures or anything. She was kind of teaching herself.'

'I see. And, do you remember what she read?' said Munro. 'What she wanted to study?'

'In-between tidying the bookshelves, you mean?' said Parkes. 'Anything to do with anatomy. *Pathology for Dummies*, that kind of thing.'

'And that was trouble?'

'No, the dealing was the trouble,' said Parkes.

'Dealing?'

'She used to peddle grass, you know, weed, and a few other bits, too. Practically supplied the entire university.'

'But surely that's not enough to make her...'

'She ran a book, Inspector; credit. For all those poor, hard-up students. Thing is, she didn't charge interest on the debts, they just had to pay up when it was due, otherwise...'

'Otherwise?' said Munro.

'Let's just say a lot of students lost a lot of possessions, jewellery, stereos, phones, anything she could flog. Nine times out of ten, whatever she got was worth a lot more than the dope.'

'And she got away with it? I mean, these students, they just willingly handed over...?'

'The consequences didn't bear thinking about,' said Parkes, lowering her voice. 'She knew people, if you know what I mean.'

'I see. I do,' said Munro. 'And you knew her well enough to speak to? Or just...'

'Obviously, I was partial to a bit of weed back then. We got on okay, for what it was worth, until...'

'Until?'

'She turned on me.'

'And why would that be?' said Munro.

'Jealousy,' said Parkes. 'I had a job lined up before I graduated, that, and... and the fact it was me who turned her in.'

'Turned her in? You mean, you told the police what she was up to?'

'Yes. She was becoming too much of a nuisance, I wasn't going to stand by and watch all these kids get fleeced by...'

'And then? What happened then?' said Munro.

'Nothing much,' said Parkes. 'She got a slap on the wrist and a fine. Following week, she was at it again.'

Munro grabbed a pen and held it, poised above his notepad.

'Listen, Annabel, you've been most helpful, really, and I thank you for that, there's just one more thing. A name. I need a name.'

Parkes went silent for moment. Munro heard a sharp intake of breath.

'The Leen,' she said with a heavy sigh.

'I beg your pardon?'

'The Leen. That's what they called her. Aileen.'

'Aileen who?'

'Wish I knew.'

West looked on in silence as Munro lowered his pen and gently placed the receiver on the cradle. He stood, slowly stretched, and reached for his coat.

'You heard that?' he said.

'I got the gist of it,' said West. 'At least we have a name.'

'A name, Charlie. Singular. We need two, the second one being more important. Have a word with Tommy, see if he can't find something on this Aileen lassie, start with the local force by the university; if she was taken in, they'll have a surname.'

'If she was taken in, and she was dealing, it was probably false.'

'We'll see,' said Munro. 'We'll see. You look tired, are you not hungry?'

West smiled.

'I'm famished,' she said. 'I'll grab something on the way home.'

'No, no. Come with me. I know a wee place across the green.'

* * *

Alberto, surprised at the sight of Munro entering the restaurant with a companion, hastily set the table for two and dressed it with a carnation in an empty Orangina bottle.

'James!' he said, sporting a grin normally reserved for his youngest daughter, hands clasped beneath his chin. 'And-a who is this-a beautiful lady? Is-a your daughter, no? Your-a niece, maybe?'

Munro regarded him from beneath a furrowed brow and spoke quietly.

'She's in custody,' he said, flatly. 'In three hours, she'll be deported.'

'Oh,' said Alberto, snatching the carnation from the table. 'Is-a shame. You-a still wanna some wine?'

'Bottle, please. Two glasses.'

West tossed her coat on the banquette and eyed Alberto, in his starched, white shirt and slicked-back hair, flirtatiously.

'Dinnae think about it, lassie,' said Munro, as he sat. 'He's married. Five bairns.'

West lowered her head and smiled.

111

'You know me too well,' she said.

'Better than you think, Charlie. Better than you think. Will you take some wine, or would you prefer the usual?'

'I'm sorry?'

'Vodka, unless I'm mistaken. You know, the great thing about vodka is the fact that it's odourless. It's the jakey's tipple of choice.'

West grabbed a menu.

'Wine's fine,' she said, cheeks flushing. 'Just fine.'

Alberto returned, poured the Barolo and, having never served a felon before, stood cautiously by Munro.

'So,' he said, doing his utmost to appear normal, 'tonight James, you're-a going to surprise me. Tonight, you wanna try-a something-a new and exciting, something that make-a your mouth say "I'm in-a heaven", no?'

'No,' said Munro. 'Steak, please.'

'Steak. It's-a wonder you don't-a look like-a cow. And-a for the beautiful signorina?'

West glanced down the menu, tracing the list of mains with her index finger.

'I'll have...' she said hesitating, nervously. 'I'll have the aubergine, the grilled aubergine with parmesan, and a tomato salad, please. Tomato and feta.'

Munro laughed aloud, grabbed Alberto by the wrist to prevent him leaving, and stared at West. She raised her eyebrows, momentarily stumped.

'Alright,' she said, caving in. 'Alright, alright. I'll have the same as him. Steak. Big one. Do you have chips?'

Alberto sighed.

'We don't have-a the chips, signorina, we have-a the patatine fritte.'

'Chips?'

'Si.'

'Good. Lots. Thanks.'

West took a healthy glug of wine, followed by another, and sat back.

112

'I must be made of glass,' she said, 'cos you can see right through me.'

Munro smiled but said nothing.

'So, what brought you down here?' said West. 'What made the south so irresistibly alluring to the monarch of the glen?'

Munro paused before answering.

'My wife,' he said, sipping his wine.

'God, you're a dark horse, aren't you? Never even knew you were married. Where is she? At home?'

'She's dead.'

West drained her glass and reached for the bottle.

'Well, that's a conversation stopper, if ever there was one,' she said, shocked by his blunt reply. 'Sorry. I didn't... well, you wouldn't, would you? I mean...'

'It's okay, Charlie,' said Munro. 'Really. Calm yourself. You'll ruin your appetite.'

West smiled.

'What happened?' she said softly. 'Was it down here? You moved down here and...'

'No, no. I came here afterwards. I had to... breathe again.'

'I don't understand,' said West.

'I was suffocating, Charlie. Jean was... she was... it wasn't, natural causes.'

'What? You mean she was...'

'Arson,' said Munro.

'Arson? Fuck. You're kidding. Why?'

'Someone wasn't keen on my... lines of inquiry.'

'Shit. I am so sorry. Truly. But, hold on, if it was arson, surely that means her death would be...'

'Murder? Aye. It was murder,' said Munro.

'Did you catch them?'

'Oh, I caught them, Charlie.'

'Well, I hope they got life,' said West.

'Longer than that, lassie,' said Munro. 'Longer than that.'

West fiddled with a breadstick, clearly not intent on eating it.

'It must be lonely,' she said compassionately. 'I mean, being so far from home and... I mean, you must miss her.'

'Every waking hour,' said Munro. 'But I'm getting used to it. I'm content, now. I'm happy in my own company. Unlike you.'

'Me?' said West. 'What do you mean? I'm fine...'

'Och, Charlie, come clean, lassie,' said Munro. 'You cannae fool me. Someone your age shouldnae be alone. Do you not have a suitor?'

West smiled, warmed by Munro's antiquated use of English.

'No,' she said. 'I... there was someone, once, but...'

'I'll not pry into your past, lassie, least said.'

'It's alright, just didn't work out, that's all. It was my fault, I'm too, selfish. Too...'

'Don't say career-minded. Your nose will grow.'

West smirked.

'I'd like to be. Career-minded, that is, it's just that sometimes I wonder if I, you know...'

'You made the right decision?'

'Yeah. The problem with me is, see, I hanker after things and, as soon as I get them, I'm bored. I have a habit of screwing things up. Spoiled brat, right?'

Munro drained his glass as the steaks arrived.

'You're running from yourself, Charlie. No-one else,' he said. 'Stop running and you'll get there.'

CHAPTER 13

"WHO IS SHE?"

She. Is the tingle.

The frisson. The spark.

She is the flame to your third-degree burns.

She is the hunger that riddles your gut, the insomnia that steals your sleep.

She's the pea beneath the mattress, the stone in your shoe, the itch you cannot reach.

She's virulent. Infectious. Debilitating. Pernicious.

She is a walking contradiction.

She is as beautiful as the dawn, and as dark as the night.

She's the opposite of good, and the antithesis of evil.

She is as loving as she is loveless.

As vulnerable as she is confident.

As capricious as she is predictable.

As faithful as she is perfidious.

As deadly as she is healing.

She's the girl who was betrayed.

The girl who vowed revenge.

She's the girl you always look for. And hope you never find.

CHAPTER 14

OSPRINGE HOUSE, WOOTTON STREET, SE1.
7:18am
West, caught between pity and sympathy, and a spiteful sense of triumph, gloated at the sorry sight before her. It was not the Samantha Baker she'd derided 24 hours earlier. Gone was the youthful complexion, the immaculate hair, the bespoke outfit and the radiant smile. She stared, instead, at a dishevelled woman approaching middle age, clad only in a knee length tee-shirt; her skin, dry; her hair, bedraggled; and her eyes, a glassy shade of red.

'You again?' said Baker, tossing a reefer onto the street. 'You'd better come in.'

The lounge, curtains pulled tight, was dark and cold. A pungent mix of cigarette smoke and cannabis hung heavy in the air. An ashtray, full to overflowing, spilled its contents across the table.

'Drink?' said Baker as she sat and shook a cigarette from the pack. 'Oh. No milk. Sorry. Unless you want black. Or water.'

Munro smiled appreciatively.

'Nothing, thanks,' he said softly, gesturing towards the chair. 'May I?'

Samantha nodded.

'So,' she said. 'What is it this time?'

Munro paused before answering.

'How are you feeling?' he said with all the grace of an undertaker.

'Fine. Numb, to be honest,' said Baker. 'A bit numb.'

'To be expected,' said Munro.

'Do you have someone who could come over?' said West in a faux display of compassion. 'You shouldn't be alone at a time like this, we could arrange…'

Baker sneered, her voice low and vindictive.

'You don't know anything about grief, do you Sergeant?' she said. 'If you did, you'd know this is precisely the time I need to be alone, not smothered by some fawning, do-gooder asking me if I'm alright and plying me with endless cups of tea.'

'Look, I'm sure you'd rather be left in peace,' said Munro, 'so I'll be as brief as possible. As you know…'

'You're trying to…'

'Indeed. So, tell me, Miss Baker, I was wondering, would you ever have cause to visit Islington, at all? Say, Upper Street, perhaps?'

'What? Islington? No, of course not,' said Baker, billowing smoke towards the ceiling.

'You're sure? No friends, work colleagues…?'

'Positive.'

'How about Richmond?' said Munro, his words now tumbling faster than a game of snap.

'No.'

'Pimlico?'

'What is this?'

'Epping?'

'Epping?'

'How about Wanstead?'

'Wanstead? Ah, now that's where…'

Baker stopped abruptly. Her eyes darted towards West, then back to the table. She huffed as she stubbed out the cigarette.

'I mean...'

'You were seen,' said Munro softly. 'Clock Court.'

'You must be mistaken,' said Baker. 'Never heard of it.'

'Och, come now,' said Munro, sighing as though he were bored with the whole charade. 'We know you were there. A police officer witnessed you arriving. 8:45am. Which, coincidentally, is little more than an hour after we left you.'

Baker, lighting another cigarette, glared at Munro and said nothing.

'Okay, lassie,' he said. 'I give up. You can either tell us what you know about Harry, here and now, or you can dress yourself and we'll run you over to our place for a wee chat. Which will it be?'

Baker cradled her head in her hands, rubbed her eyes and surrendered gracefully.

'Alright,' she said, wearily. 'Alright. I was there. Clock Court. I went to... I don't know why I went. Harry and I, we were... we were seeing each other. Always have been. Never stopped, in fact. I always hoped one day we might... forget it. It was nothing serious. Well, he didn't think so, anyway. But that's Harry for you. He never took anything seriously.'

'Thank you,' said Munro. 'I appreciate your honesty. So, when did you see him last?'

'Don't know. About a week ago, I think. I've lost track of time, I can't...'

'Nae bother,' said Munro, taking the frame from West and placing it on the table. 'Look at this wee photo again, would you, at the lassie there. Are you sure you don't know her?'

'Positive,' said Baker. 'No idea, and before you ask again, it's still not Annabel.'

Munro paused, leaned back in his chair and drummed his fingers on the table.

'I see you... I see you still enjoy a wee smoke,' he said.

'What of it?' said Baker. 'It's not illegal.'

'No, no, but forgive me, I'm a wee bit confused. You see, this lassie here, she used to frequent your campus. In fact, she was virtually the sole supplier of, you know, weed, grass, call it what you will. That being the case, I'm really quite surprised you don't recognise her.'

'No surprise, Inspector,' said Baker. 'I never went near a dealer; I got my gear from Annabel. She bought it for me.'

'Fair enough,' said Munro. 'Tell me, did you... did you know that Harry was betrothed? That is to say, married?'

'No. Yes. Yes, I knew,' said Baker. 'He told me. Said he thought he'd made a mistake but it needn't change "what we had", and I believed him.'

'Perhaps I'm old-fashioned but did that not bother you? The fact that you were seeing a married man?'

'I'm not a saint,' said Baker. 'I knew I'd get my chance, eventually. What is it they say, "Marry in haste, repent at leisure"? I just had to bide my time, that's all. Until then, we made a pact, we promised never to speak of her. Or rather, I, made him promise never to speak of her. I didn't want to hear what they'd been up to on the weekends, or what a fabulous time they were having together. I don't think I could have taken the guilt. It sounds selfish, I know, but I didn't even want to know what she looked like.'

Munro leaned forward, allowing the tiniest of smiles to lift a corner of his mouth.

'Well, now's your chance,' he said, tapping the picture frame. 'That's her.'

Baker's eyes widened as she gazed, transfixed, at the photograph.

'What?' she said, exasperated. 'That's her? So that's... I was right, that is the girl he was with in Aldeburgh?'

'Aye. That's her.'

'The bastard. You're telling me they were married, back then?'

'Indeed, they were.'

'The lying little... I knew I couldn't trust him. I bloody knew it. You know, he never said a word, not a bloody word, not till... oh, what does it matter? Really, what the f–? Nothing matters, now, does it?'

She lowered her eyes.

'She's very pretty,' she said solemnly. 'Was. Was pretty. For a terrier.'

Munro stood and zipped up his jacket.

'Well, we'll leave you be, Miss Baker,' he said. 'For what it's worth, I'm sorry. For your loss. Really.'

Baker forced a smile.

'Thanks,' she said. 'Can I ask, the funeral, I'd like to...'

'That'll be for the Farnsworth-Browns to arrange,' said Munro. 'We'll ask them to keep you informed. Oh, I almost forgot; one last thing, shoes.'

'I beg your pardon?'

'Shoes. Where do you keep them? Something we need to check, then we can be on our way.'

Baker sighed.

'Through there,' she said, pointing towards the bedroom. 'Bottom of the wardrobe. Take your pick.'

West disappeared and returned a few moments later, shaking her head.

* * *

'Well?' said Munro as they headed for the car.

'Two pairs of court shoes,' said West, 'one pair of boots, pair of flat pumps and about a million pairs of killer heels.'

'So, no Converse?'

'Nope.'

'We can rule her out, then. A liar and a philanderer she may be, but a killer, she is not.'

'So, what now?' said West.

'Back to base. You've a phone call to make.'

'I have?'

'The Farnsworth-Browns. It's about time they knew about Harry.'

'Me? But, I've never…'

'First time for everything, Charlie. First time for everything.'

* * *

Munro cast a sideways glance at West, clicked his fingers and pointed to the telephone. She slumped in her chair and reluctantly began dialling.

'Tommy,' he said, 'have you spoken to Jeff? Is there any…'

'Guv. They've got a formal ID. It's Jason Chan, alright.'

'And the prints? Any dabs apart from Mr Chan's?'

'Nothing, guv,' said Tommy. 'Place is as clean as a whistle. Must have the same cleaner as our Harry.'

'I've no doubt about that, Tommy. No doubt, at all. How about the chaps in Nottingham, did they have anything on this Aileen lassie and her entrepreneurial activities?'

Cole laughed.

'Make her sound like she's businesswoman of the year,' he said. 'But no. They reckon she wasn't charged, otherwise they'd have her on file.'

'Well, that tallies with Parkes' story, anyway.'

'Besides, for something like that, they said they probably wouldn't bother, got bigger fish to fry.'

'Have they, indeed?' said Munro. 'They should see the one we've landed.'

'Got time for a brew, or you off out again?' said Cole.

'Out. But we'll not be long.'

West was surprisingly chirpy as she hung up the phone.

'Well?' said Munro.

'Done,' she said, standing to remove her jacket. 'I spoke to Ed Farnsworth-Brown, he was, well, almost not bothered. I mean, didn't sound shocked, no outbursts, no…'

'That's Americans for you, Charlie. Far too relaxed about everything. Including death. It'll hit him later. Leave your coat on, we're away, just now.'

'Where?'

'Delgado. I assume he's not answered your calls?'

'No, but…'

'And you have an address?'

'Yes, but…'

'Then let's go.'

'Can't we sit down for five minutes? Quick cup of…'

The door slammed as Munro hurtled down the stairs.

'Never mind, miss,' said Tommy, smiling. 'I'll have one waiting for you when you get back.'

* * *

School run over, dogs walked and post delivered, Halstead Road, with its rows of terraced workers' cottages, was as quiet as a Cumbrian hill pass. Munro parked up directly outside Delgado's house and killed the engine.

'That was hardly worth the drive,' said West. 'We could have walked.'

'Right enough,' said Munro. 'But if he's not in, we'll need somewhere to sit.'

'Suppose so.'

'Well, off you go.'

West rang the bell and waited. She rang again, rapped the door knocker like an irate courier, then stepped back and glanced at the upstairs windows, as if it might hasten a response.

'He's out,' she said, slamming the car door.

'You don't say.'

'Shall we go?'

'No, no. We'll wait a while,' said Munro.

123

'Looks a bit odd, doesn't it?'

'What does?'

'This,' said West. 'You and me, sitting in a car, doing nothing.'

'What would you like to do?'

'I don't know, maybe we should be… I don't know. God, we could be here for hours. Nothing to drink, no food. We could starve to death…'

'Something troubling you, Charlie?' said Munro. 'You appear to be irritated, and I find that somewhat irritating. Is there a problem?'

'No. Sorry,' said West, 'just hungry, that's all. Starving, in fact. Blood sugar must be low, plus, I'm due in a day or… oh, God, too much information, sorry.'

Munro, chest heaving as he chuckled silently in his seat, reached in his pocket and pulled out a bar of Kendal Mint Cake.

'Here,' he said, 'eat this. I always keep one handy, just in case I'm caught short, too. It's got so much sugar in it, you'll be on the ceiling for a week.'

'Thanks,' said West, stuffing her face. 'It's disgusting. Do you think we'll be here much longer?'

'No. I'd say about, oh, a minute, or thereabouts.'

'A minute? Very funny, what makes you…'

'Because, if I'm not mistaken, this is the chappie we've been waiting for.'

Delgado, struggling with a large, blank canvas clamped beneath one arm and a holdall in the other, ambled towards them. Attired, as he was, in a black pea-coat with a flat cap perched on the back of his head and a cigarette dangling from his lips, he looked more like a Catalan docker than an artist.

'He,' said West, lowering her voice as if divulging some tawdry piece of illicit information, 'is unnaturally good-looking.'

Munro shook his head and tutted.

'What?' she said. 'Look, if he's innocent, I'm not going to let that go to waste... I may give him a... shit, he's seen us.'

Delgado smiled through the windscreen as he approached the gate. Munro acknowledged the greeting with a polite nod of the head.

'That's torn it,' said West, 'what do we do now? He knows...'

'He knows nothing, lassie. Probably thinks we're bailiffs, or Immigration, or, God forbid, in the throes of a clandestine affair.'

Munro craned his neck and watched intently as Delgado dropped his holdall to the floor, fumbled in his pocket and retrieved a set of keys.

'Have you heard of a Mati?' he said, drawing a breath as he flicked the ignition.

'A what? No.'

'I'll explain later, but you can cancel any plans you have concerning our friend, here. If I'm not mistaken, he won't be dating anyone for a very long time.'

'What are you talking about?' said West. 'Honestly, sometimes... I thought the whole point of us coming here was to speak to...'

'It was, but that was then. We'll come back in a while.'

'I don't follow. Why not now? We're only going to...'

'Because,' said Munro, 'we might need some help. I've a terrible feeling this Delgado chappie is more involved than we thought.'

* * *

'Guv,' said Cole impatiently, as West and Munro returned to the office. 'I've been trying to call you; we've got a...'

'Tommy, Tommy, Tommy, will you calm yourself,' said Munro. 'What is it? Have you won the lottery?'

'No.'

'Have you found yourself a girlfriend?'

'Er, no.'

'Then first things first. Remove coat, boil kettle, make tea. Oh, and I'll take a biscuit, if we have any. Then we can sit down and have a chat while Charlie, here, has forty winks. She's frail from hunger, the poor thing.'

West smiled as Cole hurriedly brewed a couple of mugs, split a packet of Cheddars in two and plonked them on their respective desks. Munro sighed.

'There's an art to making tea, Tommy, it requires time and patience, qualities, I fear, you're lacking in spades. Now, what is it?'

'We've got another…'

'Yes, yes, I gathered that. Another what?'

'Missing person,' said Cole.

Munro turned to the window, bit into a biscuit and took a slurp of scalding tea.

'Carry on like this, and we'll soon be twinned with El Salvador. Who is it this time? Teen? Male? Female?'

'Woman, late twenties…'

'Do we have a name?'

Cole checked his notes.

'Miss Hannah Lawson,' he said.

'How long?'

'Two days.'

'Och, she's not missing,' said Munro. 'She's lost.'

'I know, guv, but they say it's…'

'They?'

'Her boss, where she works; library on Vestry…'

'Is she on our patch?'

'Yes, guv, Cowley Road,' said Cole.

'Okay,' said Munro, 'if we must. Nip downstairs, send a couple of constables round, tell them to do the usual, see if anyone's home, check with the neighbours, get a statement from her employers, then get straight back; you're coming with us, in civvies, if you please. Chop, chop.'

* * *

Halstead Road was experiencing a minor resurgence in activity as the first tranche of school kids, gorging on bags of chips and family-sized packs of Doritos, slowly made their way home. Sergeant Cole, having parked half a dozen car lengths behind Munro, shook his head despondently as he watched them amble by. His radio crackled.

'Guv,' he said into his collar.

'Tommy, we're going to have a word with this Delgado fellow, now. Once we're done, we'll be away around the corner but you're to wait, understand? When he goes out, you're to follow, discreetly mind, on foot. He'll not be driving. Got that?'

'Guv.'

West looked scornfully at Munro.

'What?'

'You do realise I'm losing weight because of you?' she said.

'It's not me,' said Munro. 'It's all that raw fish you eat. It's not healthy.'

* * *

Delgado, thought West, looked even more alluring out of his coat. Her eyes fluttered as he opened the door wearing just a white, sleeveless vest and jeans.

'Hello again,' he said, snapping through an apple.

'Again?' said West, smiling coyly.

'You were outside earlier, sitting in the car.'

'Oh, that. We were… we were just…'

'Plucking up the courage to come in?' said Delgado, with a grin. 'You needn't have waited, you know, I don't bite, especially when there's an attractive lady involved.'

'Good grief,' said Munro, waving his warrant card. 'Any more lines like that and I shall jettison my breakfast all over your door. Police officers. May we?'

Delgado stepped aside, winked at West and ushered them in with a theatrical wave of the arm.

'Detective Inspector Munro, and this is Detective Sergeant West.'

'Really? And does D.S. West have a first name?'

'Desperate,' said Munro. 'Now, a wee word, if we may; it's about Harry Farns…'

'Harry? What's up?'

'He's not been seen for a few days; some folk are concerned for his… safety.'

'Wouldn't worry about that,' said Delgado. 'Harry often disappears for a day or two. He's probably fleecing some rich divorcée on the Côte d'Azur, as we speak.'

'Is that so? And why would he disappear like that? Is he one for travelling?'

'Good Lord, no,' said Delgado. 'He likes his home comforts too much. He's prone to bouts of depression, that's all, nothing too serious. Been like that ever since he lost Annabel. Goes away to clear his head, that sort of thing.'

'And he always comes back?'

'Well, obviously,' said Delgado.

'Indulge me, would you?' said Munro. 'D.S. West, here, has something to show you.'

'Best offer I've had all day.'

'You're making my skin crawl, laddie.'

West, cheeks flushing, swiped her phone and showed Delgado the shot of Harry.

'Do you recognise these people?' she said sternly, trying to sound officious.

'Well, of course, gosh, that was taken a while back, wasn't it?'

'I'm waiting,' said West.

'Sorry, it's Harry and Annabel.'

'Annabel?' said Munro.

'Sure, his wife.'

'It's not Aileen?'

'Aileen?'

'Doesn't matter,' said Munro. 'Tell me, if Harry was going away, to clear his head, so to speak, is there anyone he may call, to let them know?'

'Ooh, no, not really,' said Delgado. 'Harry isn't big on friends. Oh, Sam, maybe. He might have called Sam.'

'Sam?'

'Sammy. Samantha, thick as thieves, those two.'

'Would this be Samantha Baker?' said Munro.

'One and the same. If you ask me, he should've married her instead, opposites and all that.'

'Is that so?'

'Just an opinion, nothing against Annabel, she was absolutely delightful; cute, little thing but very, intense. Serious. Enjoyed flirting, though.'

'Flirting? That sounds a little out of character, wouldn't you say?' said West.

'Maybe. Maybe it was just me, but it always seemed like, given half the chance…'

'Nothing wrong with your ego, is there, Mr Delgado?'

'Well, if you've got it, Sergeant.'

'This Samantha Baker,' said Munro. 'Know her well, do you?'

'In a way, not that we've ever met, but Harry's always banging on about her. I think it would do him good, you know, if he and she… I mean, it's been a while since Annabel… new beginnings and all that.'

'And Annabel,' said Munro. 'Do you recall the last time you saw her?'

'Blimey, eons. Just before they got married, I think, so that would be a good couple of months before she… you know.'

'And you didnae go to the wedding? Not best man, or…'

'No, wasn't asked, they slipped away and did it quietly, just came back and said "surprise, we're married".'

'And that didn't strike you as odd?' said Munro.

'Not really,' said Delgado. 'For a start, Harry can be a bit impulsive; plus, the way I see it, there's only two reasons people get married that quickly, one is love, and the other involves a shotgun. Neither of them owns a firearm, and I don't think she was pregnant, so...'

'And Harry's parents, do you...'

'Nah. I only see them if Harry's there and he invites me over. Apart from that...'

'Okay, well, that should do for now. Oh, just one thing, did Harry ever mention anyone called Mati?'

'You mean, like, Matthew?'

'Aye, maybe, but spelt m-a-t-i.'

'That's not a name, Inspector, it's a symbol, a sort of, charm.'

'Is it, indeed?' said Munro, as if genuinely surprised. 'Well, well, well. I think we've taken up enough of your time Mr Delgado, if you hear anything, don't be afraid to give us a wee call.'

'I will,' said Delgado, grinning at West. 'And you, can call me anytime.'

* * *

'Well, we didn't get much out of that, did we?' groaned West as her eyes caught sight of the blackboard outside The Nightingale.

'Oh, I'd say you got quite a lot out of it, Charlie, quite a lot, indeed. Worry not, the seeds, as they say, have been sown.'

'Working with a bloody farmer, now,' said West. 'Cumberland sausage and mash.'

'What's that?' said Munro.

'Sausage and mash, or homemade lasagne. We could nip in for a quick...'

'No, no, Tommy will be calling soon enough, trust me. Besides, I thought you'd become a fan of The Duke, why would you not want to eat there?'

'Oh, no reason. Let's just say the staff are... over-rated.'

A steady stream of early evening regulars, comprising cabbies and after-workers too raw from their commute to face the tedium of home, flowed into the pub. West, bored, tired and hungry, swiped her phone for the umpteenth time and whined like a six-year-old about to throw a tantrum.

'For God's sake,' she said. 'One hour and fourteen minutes, we've been here. One hour, fourteen minutes. So much for Delgado going out, Sergeant Cole's probably fallen asleep, I'm dying of thirst and my bum hurts. I have to stretch my legs, I'm getting cramp, I might just wander over...'

'Haud yer wheesht, lassie,' said Munro.

'What? Haud yer, what?'

'Stop blethering,' said Munro, retrieving his mobile. 'It's Tommy. Tommy?'

'Guv, he left a couple of minutes ago. I've followed him and this is, well, it's a bit weird, to be honest.'

'What is, Tommy? For goodness sake...'

'Well, he's not gone far,' said Cole. 'In fact, he's in a house on Cowley Road. The house where that girl lives, the one reported missing earlier, from the library.'

'You're sure?'

'Dead sure, I'm right outside.'

'Hold tight, Tommy,' said Munro, firing up the engine. 'Do not let him out of your sight, we'll be there in 30 seconds.'

* * *

Lights off, Munro eased the car along Cowley Road until he spotted Cole loitering beneath a lamp post, looking, to all intents and purposes, like a prospective burglar.

'Couldn't be less obvious if he was wearing camouflage. Right,' he said, turning to West. 'Charlie, two things, wait here and keep the engine running. I'll take Tommy with me, in case he gets a bit, you know. Second, here's my phone, find the number for a Doctor Jackie Banham…'

'Doctor?' said West. 'Are you…?'

'She's used to talking to people with criminal tendencies. Ask her if she wouldn't mind coming in. Something tells me she could prove somewhat invaluable.'

'I don't get it; why would you ask a…'

'Okay, Charlie, remember I mentioned the Mati?'

'Yes…'

'It's a symbol, I'll not go into detail, suffice to say, Delgado has one on his keychain.'

'So?'

'The photographs of Harry, the ones we found on the phone? The same key chain was lying on the bed.'

'You think…'

'Maybe. Lock the doors.'

* * *

'My, my, this is a surprise,' said Delgado, still wearing his coat and hat. 'Didn't expect to see you again, quite so soon, Inspector.'

'No, I'm sure not,' said Munro. 'And I didn't realise you were into property, Mr Delgado, how many houses do you own in the area?'

Delgado laughed politely.

'Very good, Inspector,' he said. 'But one mortgage is enough for me.'

'Then perhaps you could tell me what, exactly, you're doing here?'

'Of course, come in, come in. I'm what you might call, house sitting, sort of.'

'Sort of?' said Munro, rattled by Delgado's relaxed demeanour.

'What I mean is, I'm not staying here. I pop in now and then, to keep an eye on things.'

'I see.'

'You say that as if it sounds odd,' said Delgado. 'I can assure you, Inspector, it's all above board.'

Munro said nothing. He peered upstairs before wandering, slowly, into the front room.

'And how long is your friend away?' he said, scanning the bookshelves.

'Oh, just a few days,' said Delgado. 'She'll be...'

'She?'

'Yes.'

'A few days, you say? Where has she gone?'

'Ooh, couldn't say; don't know, I'm afraid. Friends, I imagine.'

'Perhaps she's gone to clear her head?' said Munro.

'I'm sorry?'

'You said Mr Farnsworth-Brown often goes away to clear his head, so I wondered...'

'Oh, I see what you mean,' said Delgado. 'No, she doesn't need to do that and, before you ask, she doesn't suffer from depression either. She's rather enlightened. Enjoys a positive outlook on...'

'Good,' said Munro. 'Then, she'll not be upset to find us here when she gets back. I assume you know when she's coming back?'

Delgado pushed back his cap, scratched his head and smiled nervously.

'Actually, I... you know, I don't, exactly, she said she'd...'

'And does she have a name?' said Munro. 'This friend of yours, the one who trusts you enough to give you her house keys?'

'She does,' said Delgado. 'Problem is, I, er, I just don't know it.'

Munro walked to the window and pulled the blinds shut.

'It's getting dark out,' he said. 'Folk can see in. So, let's get this straight, you've let yourself in to a young lady's house using her very own set of door keys and you've no idea of her name or where she's gone? Do you not think that sounds a wee bit odd?'

'Well, if you put it like that, I suppose…'

'It sounds downright unbelievable, laddie…'

'She told me... she told me,' said Delgado, 'the less we knew about each other, the better it would be. That, if we got too involved, we might end up…'

'Are you intimate with her?' said Munro. 'I mean, you and her, are you in a relationship?'

'Yes, if I'm honest…'

'And that's not involved?'

Delgado, looking embarrassed, drove his hands into his pockets and sighed.

'Look, to be blunt,' he said, 'our relationship is basically, well, physical. Nothing more. We shag. Okay?'

'I believe there's an app for that,' said Munro as he ambled to the kitchen. He stood, stock still, closed his eyes and, head tilted back, took a long, deep breath. 'Bleach,' he said, quietly.

Delgado glanced at Cole and shrugged his shoulders.

'I cleaned up a bit,' he said.

Munro, his attention focused on the sink, spoke without moving.

'Your friend's away,' he said softly. 'You're not stopping here, you've clearly not eaten here, and yet, you "cleaned up a bit"?'

'That's right. I hate mess, Inspector. I like everything to be neat and tidy.'

'So do I, Mr Delgado,' said Munro, spinning on his heels, hand outstretched, 'so do I. Keys, if you please. The ones with the Mati on the chain.'

Delgado raised his eyebrows in shock as he reached in his pocket.

'Mati?' he said. 'You've been leading me on, haven't you, Inspector? You knew what it was all along. You are clever, only thing is, it's not mine. It's hers, they're her keys, for here.'

Munro, scratching his nose and frowning, made his way back to the lounge.

'I've a wee problem, here, Mr Delgado,' he said. 'You see, as far-fetched as your story sounds, it could, at a stretch, be construed as believable. Thing is, I don't believe it, and the young lady's employers have reported her as missing.'

'Missing? Well, she obviously forgot to tell them she was going away. Silly thing.'

'Aye. Possibly. But unlikely, wouldn't you say?'

'I…'

'I think we need to spend some time together, you and I. I've a few more questions I'd like to ask. Would you mind coming with us?'

'What? You mean… are you charging me with something? Are you arresting…'

'No, no, no,' said Munro, shaking his head. 'Just a wee chat, that's all. Of course, if you'd rather not join us now, I could always…'

'Nope, that's fine,' said Delgado. 'Happy to. Shall we?'

* * *

The sound of heavy boots, rapidly thumping their way up the wooden staircase, was adequate warning of Sergeant Cole's imminent, but nonetheless, unsettling, arrival. West shuddered as he burst through the door sporting a satisfied grin on his face.

'That's our guest tucked up for the night, guv,' he said. 'All sounds a bit rum, don't you think? Him in that house, I mean.'

'It does indeed, Tommy,' said Munro, settling into his seat.

'What shall we…'

'The first thing we must do, Tommy, is attend to Detective Sergeant West, here.'

'Come again? I don't…'

'Can you not see the poor lassie's wasting away?' said Munro. 'There's nothing left of her. Charlie, I know you're weak with hunger but would you be offended if I asked you to fetch us all some supper? You being a fussy eater, I imagine...'

'Bloody love to,' said West, leaping from her desk. 'What do you want, quick, before I faint.'

'You choose,' said Munro. 'As long as there's no garlic. Or chillies, or onions, or peppers, and nothing spicy, mind, like Indian or Chinese or...'

'Chippy it is, then.'

'Aye, a fish supper. That would be most agreeable. Now, I'm not keen on cod, or skate, nor plaice. I'll have the haddock, please, and no vinegar on the chips. You could get yourself some deep-fried sushi.'

'Ha. Ha. Sergeant Cole?'

'Very kind, miss. Saveloy and chips, do me fine.'

Munro stood by the window and smiled as he watched West sprint across the green to the High Street.

'I bet she's not done that on the beat, eh, Tommy?'

'Unlikely, guv. Here's the file from the lads downstairs, the ones who made the enquiries about Hannah Lawson.'

'Most efficient. Convey my thanks when you see them next.'

'They said they got a picture too, from the library, it's the same shot they used on her ID card.'

'Right, let's take a look shall we, I wonder... Jumping Jehoshaphat, have you seen this?'

'No, guv, not had a chance.'

Munro took the photograph from the file and passed it over.

'Remind you of anyone?' he said.

'Bloody hell! Looks just like Parkes. If it ain't, it's her bleedin' double, guv, talk about dead ringers. Anything else in there?'

Munro leafed through the pages, humming and shaking his head.

'No. No. No, all seems perfectly normal. Even down to the fact that she never talked to her neighbours. That's society for you these days, Tommy. Folk are more interested in their phones than their fellow man. Could be dead in your bed for a week and no-one would bat an eyelid.'

'I think the dog would bark a bit,' said Cole. 'When he realised he wasn't getting any dinner, like.'

'Speaking of which.'

West hurriedly doled out the soggy, paper-wrapped parcels and pulled three bottles from her jacket pockets.

'I got us a beer too,' she said. 'If that's alright, sir. Just one each, it's low alcohol, Mexican stuff, only 4%, you won't get…'

'Thank you, Charlie,' said Munro, 'that's very thoughtful of you. Before you sit down…'

'Oh, what now?'

'Nothing, just take a look at that wee photograph Tommy has in his hand. Tell me what you think.'

'Well, it's obvious isn't it?' said West, as she stuffed a chip in her mouth. 'It's Annabel Parkes. Where'd you get it? The Farnsworth-Browns?'

'The library.'

'Don't follow.'

'That, is Hannah Lawson.'

Sergeant Cole reached for the bottle opener as West, doing her best to swallow a piping-hot chip, coughed and spluttered, hoping no-one would attempt the Heimlich manoeuvre.

'Holy crap,' she said, glugging back the beer. 'Are you serious? Really?'

'Really,' said Munro, returning to the window. 'Eat up, afore it gets cold.'

'But guv…'

West held a finger to her lips, instructing Cole to remain silent, as Munro, lost in thought, picked half-heartedly at his fish supper. Staring into the black, night sky, he waited, patiently, until they'd finished eating before taking a sip of beer and speaking.

'Here is a theory for you,' he said. 'This Annabel Parkes. We know she wasn't what you might call fun-loving by nature; in fact, by all accounts, she was quite the opposite. Serious. Dour, even. And Samantha Baker likened her to a terrier, which suggests she also had a jealous side. Intensely jealous. So, let's imagine for moment that she knew about Harry and Miss Baker's affair. Let's say she knew they were seeing each other behind her back. Why, she'd be enraged, would she not? Furious. Beside herself with anger. But what could she do? Leave him? File for divorce? Not the ideal solution for someone who's insanely jealous. Why? Because that would leave him free to pursue his other love interest.'

'You mean,' said West, enthralled by Munro's storytelling, 'you mean, if I can't have him, nobody can, kind of thing?'

'Aye. Exactly. So... so what if she didn't drown in Aldeburgh, after all? What if she simply, disappeared...'

'And what?' said Cole. 'Reinvented herself as Hannah Lawson, came back and took care of Harry? Bit far-fetched, ain't it, guv?'

'Is it, Tommy?'

'Seems like a lot of trouble to go to, just to...'

'As Mrs Farnsworth-Brown said, hell hath no fury, Tommy. Hell hath no fury. Okay, assuming I'm right, let's also assume that Hannah, or Annabel, is no longer with us, and we find the body. The problem then is how do we prove who she is?'

'Easy, guv,' said Cole. 'We get a DNA profile, job done.'

'Full marks for enthusiasm, Tommy, but tell me, what do we match it to? If we're to believe what the Farnsworth-Browns tell us, she has no family.'

'Oh, yeah,' said Cole. 'Good point. Forgot about that.'

'Ah, yes, but,' said West, swigging her beer, 'no family, alive. We could do a search – births, marriages, deaths, whatever – find a next of kin, and then, even if we have to exhume a body, we could get a match.'

'You're forgetting one thing, Charlie,' said Munro as he tossed the remnants of his dinner into the wastepaper basket.

'What? What have I missed?'

'Annabel Parkes is not her real name. Who would you search for?'

'Bugger. Unless Hannah Lawson's her real name.'

'Doubtful,' said Munro, reaching for the phone. 'But we need to check. I've a quick call to make, then we're off to look at Delgado's place.'

'What?' said West. 'You can't do that, just turn up at his house and...'

'Oh, I can, and I will. I have the keys and he's not going anywhere. In fact, nip down and tell him we're a bit understaffed. May have to hold him a little longer than we anticipated. I'll meet you in the car park.'

'So much for an early night, then.'

* * *

D.I. Ashford, believing the call to be from his wife, did his best to sound suitably harassed, thereby validating his claim to be working late at the office.

'Chingford C.I.D,' he said, gruffly. 'Hold the...'

'Jeff,' said Munro. 'It's James.'

'James! Oh, thank Christ for that.'

'Are you okay?'

'Couldn't be better,' said Ashford. 'Just, er...'

'Working late?'

'In a manner of speaking. The wife's got the neighbours round, can't stand them. Should be gone by ten.'

'I see,' said Munro. 'Listen, Jeff, I need a wee favour. Have you that young laddie with you, the chap I met at Jason Chan's place?'

'You mean Sean?'

'Aye. Can you spare him?'

'What do you need?'

'Hannah Lawson. Cowley Road. Anything at all. Anything. Quick as you like.'

'No probs. Leave with and I'll give you a bell back.'

CHAPTER 15

"DID YOU LOVE HER?"

Love her? Yes, of course I loved her. I loved everything about her. We only knew each other for a short space of time but within those few weeks, I'm not ashamed to say, she became my best friend. I loved the way she smiled, that wicked 'up to no good' smile. I loved the way she was so diligent about everything she did, no half measures. I loved the way she laughed. She enjoyed laughing, it was refreshing, particularly as virtually everyone you pass on the street these days looks so... so miserable, so pissed-off. And I loved the way she smelled, the smell of her skin, her hair. Pheromones. It was a perfect match. I don't know of any smells that can send that, that tingle up your spine.

Or do you mean, was I 'in love' with her? If that's the case, then I'm not sure. Infatuated, certainly. Fond? Without a doubt. Besotted? A little, perhaps. Actually, a lot. Having said that, if I was 'in love' with her, then that would explain everything, wouldn't it? That would give me a reasonable excuse, make everything alright. I mean, people do stupid things when they're in love, don't they? Go along with anything, no matter how bad or crazy it sounds because... because love has that annoying ability to cloud one's judgement. It draws a veil over reality. Makes sense, I suppose; I mean, why else would I have got involved? Let's face it, what she got me to do was insane. Completely insane. So, maybe you're right. Maybe I was in love.

Wood. Trees. You know what I mean? When you're in that kind of situation, with someone you love, when you're in the thick of it, it's impossible to see just how bad what you're doing really is. Your conscience, your morals, your love of mankind, go clean out the window. It was like we were playing a game. Just a couple of kids playing a game together, so engrossed in what they were doing that nothing could distract them. It's like you put the outside world on pause, then, when the game's over, you pack up, go home, press play and normal life resumes. Normal life. Funny that. I don't think I know what normal is anymore. Should make for a few interesting canvases, though.

But did I love her? Yes, irrefutably.

CHAPTER 16

HALSTEAD ROAD, WANSTEAD. 8:09pm
West vaulted the stairs two at a time, paused on the landing as she counted the rooms and headed for the front bedroom. It matched her clichéd expectations of how an artist, tortured of mind and soul, might live. The floor, barely visible, was strewn with clothes destined for the washing machine, the bedside table groaned with the weight of tannin-stained teacups and half-full tumblers of water, and the walls were covered in sketches and ballpoint doodles held fast with masking tape. The bed, she decided, appeared too much of a health hazard to investigate without protective clothing. She was having second thoughts about getting 'close' with Delgado.

A cursory search of the bathroom revealed nothing out of the ordinary, no prescription medication, no blood-stained razor blades, not even a bottle of aspirin; while the back bedroom was used for storing canvases, jars of turpentine and nine-roll packs of toilet tissue. She found Munro in the rear reception room.

'Ah,' she said. 'So this is where it all happens.'

'Aye, he obviously uses this as his studio,' said Munro as he sifted through the debris on the floor with the end of a pencil. 'Anything?'

'No, clean. In a manner of speaking. Apart from his bedroom.'

'Bad?'

'I've seen worse,' said West. 'Still makes you want to shower, though.'

'So much for liking everything neat and tidy,' mumbled Munro.

'Huh?'

'Nothing. Tell me, Charlie, are all artists still... impoverished, these days?'

'Not likely,' said West. 'Make a bloody fortune, some of them.'

'Is that so? Remind me to stop by the art shop, tomorrow. I'll be needing some brushes.'

'What have you got?' she said, smirking. 'Anything we can use?'

'I'm not sure,' said Munro, pointing to an open rucksack. 'Overalls. Why would he be wanting those?'

'To protect his clothes, of course, why else?'

'Aye, I ken what you mean,' said Munro. 'But disposable ones? Even the chappie who paints the front of your house wouldnae wear these. And look here, scalpel blades...'

'Well, it's not just surgeons who use them, I mean...'

'Quite. But look here. See these on the floor, they're dirty, covered in paint or broken; it's this one that bothers me, on the handle, it's...'

'He's changed the blade,' said West. 'obviously, for a new one...'

'No, no. This blade isn't new, it's scratched and the tip's snapped off. It's been wiped clean.'

'Doesn't make sense, why clean...'

'Exactly,' said Munro, hauling himself to his feet. 'Bag it with the overalls, please Charlie, get them off to the lab, quick as you like. Tommy can do it. And tell them I need answers by the morning.'

'Got it. What now?'

'Lawson's place. I think it's time we had a wee nose around.'

* * *

The neighbour, an elderly lady who mistakenly believed the net curtains would render her invisible, watched, silhouetted by the light of her lounge as Munro searched for the right key. West smiled and waved as the door popped open, causing her to vanish from view.

'There's nothing down here,' said Munro, closing the door. 'Nothing but the stench of bleach, masking the odour of some heinous crime.'

'Bit dramatic, isn't it?' said West. 'Not to mention presumptuous.'

'Trust me, Charlie. I've a feeling about this place, and it's not a good one. Up we go.'

The bathroom was scrupulously clean. Too clean. The comparison between it and Harry's place was inevitable, with, Munro noted, one minor but significant difference. There were no personal effects. No toothbrush, no toothpaste. No shampoo, no soap, no shower gel. No towels, no sponges, no flannels.

'Hannah Lawson,' he said, joining West in the bedroom, 'is not coming back.'

'How can you be so sure?'

'I just am. What on earth are you doing?'

West, flat on her stomach, dragged herself out from under the bed.

'Cons,' she said, blowing dust from her chest. 'Four pairs. Look.'

'Size?'

'Five. And look at this left heel. Worn.'

'Bingo. Let's have them away, see if they don't match the prints from Harry's place.'

'Just the back room, then,' said West.

'It's not worth it, Charlie,' said Munro. 'We've got what we need.'

'Might as well, as we're here; only take a minute.'

The spare room, barely large enough to accommodate a single bed, was crammed with unwanted furniture and the kind of ephemera associated with moving house: an antique writing desk, an old wardrobe, plastic carrier bags stuffed with, obviously unwanted, clothes, a suitcase, a couple of lampshades and a box filled with assorted crockery and utensils.

'Junk,' said Munro. 'Come, lassie, we've work to do.'

West, ignoring his plea, rummaged through the bags like a bargain hunter at a boot sale, turning her nose up at the questionable array of patterned sweaters.

'Rubbish,' she said, turning her attention to the desk and opening the drawers one by one. 'Empty. Empty. Empty.'

As was the suitcase. She dragged the box of crockery from the front of wardrobe, managing, just, to open one door.

'Well?' said Munro, impatiently. 'Are you satisfied, now?'

'Empty,' she said, closing the door. 'Okay, we can...

She stopped, mid-sentence, glanced at Munro and stood aside.

'You'd better take a look at this.'

Munro stepped forward, heaved the crockery into the hall and swung the door open wide. Pinned to the back was a photograph of Harry, colour, old style, the kind that came from a roll of film. Next to it, a web page printed on plain paper advertising a second-hand lawnmower for sale and above that, an image of a half-naked man, oriental in appearance, slumped on a sofa.

'Chantheman,' whispered Munro. 'Thanks, Charlie.'

'What for?' said West.

'For being so stubborn. If you hadn't insisted on looking...'

'There's something else, look – behind the print of Chan, sticking out the bottom.'

Munro lifted it to reveal a newspaper clipping.

'Bloody hell,' said West. 'Is that...'

'Aye,' said Munro. 'That's me.'

'Why would she... Christ, she knew, didn't she? She knew you were on to her.'

'Either that, or she's into older men,' said Munro. 'Might have a found a nicer picture, though, don't you think?'

'So, what now?' said West. 'I mean, it's her, right? She's the one who killed...'

'Looks like it, Charlie. It certainly looks like it.'

'We need to find her, before she strikes again, put out an appeal, see if anyone's...'

'No, no,' said Munro. 'She'll not strike again, trust me. We'll do an appeal if we don't find her, but not yet. I want a word with Delgado first. Look, you get back, make sure he's comfortable and tell him I'll be there in the morning, now. Do him good to sweat a while.'

'On my way. Then what?'

'Then take yourself home, Charlie, it's been a long day. Get some rest.'

* * *

Having entrusted Sergeant Cole with the task of despatching the evidence to the lab, West fleetingly contemplated a drink in The Duke then winced at the thought of sharing her bed with someone young enough to be her son. Instead, she stopped at the newsagent, asked for a bottle of Smirnoff Red, a pack of Marlboro Lights, and rifled through her pockets in search of her purse.

'Going to have a good night?' said the man behind the counter, leering at her bust, his English, at best, pigeon. 'You make party, yes?'

West glowered at his stubble-ridden face, shaved head and tombstone teeth.

'Stuff it,' she said, turning for the door. 'I don't need it.'

CHAPTER 17

SPRATT HALL ROAD, WANSTEAD. 6:52am
'I think you've cracked him, James.'

'I beg your pardon?'

'Sean,' said D.I. Ashford. 'He's a broken man. Defeated. Been pulling his hair out all night; what there is of it.'

'I'm sorry,' said Munro, trying to remove his coat with the phone in one hand. 'You'll have to be more specific, Jeff, I've not even had my tea, yet.'

'Is your memory going? Hannah Lawson. Nothing, zilch, zero, nada. She does not exist.'

'What? But that's impossible…'

'Oh, it's possible, James. And unfortunately for you, it's true.'

'No, no,' said Munro. 'There must be something, bank account for a start, her salary has to be…'

'Not if she's not paid,' said Ashford.

'What?'

'She's a volunteer, James.'

Munro, clenching his teeth in frustration, looked to the ceiling and rubbed the back of his neck as D. I. West, looking surprisingly fresh, arrived at her desk.

'Well, what about council tax?' he said. 'Utilities, there must be...'

'Not sure if you're going to like this,' said Ashford, drawing a breath. 'But there's only one person registered at that address, and it's not her. Bloke by the name of Farnsworth-Brown, initial "hotel"...'

'What?'

'And all the bills are paid in cash, over the counter at the Post Office.'

'This smells like a trawler in Tobermory,' mumbled Munro. 'Deeds? House deeds?'

'Same.'

'You mean the house is in his name?'

'Yup.'

Munro fell silent as he struggled to find a connection between Harry, Lawson and the house.

'You still there?' said Ashford.

'Aye. Sorry, Jeff,' said Munro. 'How about the phone?'

'No landline.'

'Good grief, man; a mobile, then? She must have an account, to access the internet.'

'You know the answer to that, James,' said Ashford. 'Pay-as-you...'

'Yes, yes. Mother of God,' said Munro as the other phone rang. 'Charlie, get that will you? Jeff, is there nothing on the social? Facebook or...'

'Nothing so far. Sean'll have another pop when he wakes up but I doubt he'll get anywhere. If you ask me, this girl does not want to be found.'

'Right enough, Jeff. Right enough.'

* * *

Munro eased himself into his chair, sighed and looked at the clock.

'It's not even seven o'clock,' he said. 'I need some coffee.'

West smiled knowingly and reached for the kettle as Sergeant Cole, making his usual entrance, blew through the door.

'Blimey, guv,' he said. 'You look happy. What's up? Someone die?'

'Tommy,' said Munro, burying his head in his hands. 'I need you to make a call, quick as you can, please. The Farnsworths. See if they know anything about Hannah Lawson's place on Cowley, it's in Harry's name. Charlie, are you doing something with that kettle or just looking at it?'

'I need a word,' said West.

'And I need coffee, before I die of thirst.'

'Alright, alright,' said West, 'coming up. That call just now…'

'You'd best put an extra sugar in that.'

'That call…'

'What's the link between Lawson and Harry F?' said Munro.

'What? I don't know? Is there one? Now, that call…'

'Guv,' said Cole, hanging up the phone.

'What is it, Tommy?' said Munro.

'That gaff on Cowley, Lawson's place, it's Harry's alright. First house he bought, but his folks thought he sold it when he moved to Victory Road.'

'Well, apparently not,' said Munro.

'So how does that work?' said Cole. 'You think he was renting it to her?'

'Renting? Aye, Tommy, could be. Could… och, no. I fear it's something a wee bit darker than that. The more I think about, it, the more I'm convinced that Hannah Lawson and Annabel Parkes are one and the…'

'For crying out loud!' said West, handing him a mug.

'Calm down, Charlie, what is it?'

'I've been trying to tell you – that call just now, it was the lab. They found minute traces of DNA on that scalpel and a smidge on the overalls, on the cuffs, nothing much, but enough to...'

'Well, why didn't you say so?' said Munro. 'Standing there, fussing with the kettle, come on, don't keep it to yourself.'

'Well, there's nothing on file to match the DNA on the blade...'

'Och, Charlie, you interrupted me to tell me that? I thought you had something...'

'But the sample on the overalls...'

Munro took a deep breath and exhaled slowly.

'Yes?' he said.

West paused just long enough to rile Munro and allowed a satisfied grin to cross her face.

'The sample on the overalls, it belongs to Jason Chan,' she said.

Munro, frowning, stared at West as though he were struggling to comprehend the remark. He placed both hands palm down on the desk and slowly rose from his seat, his expression, pained.

'What's up?' said West. 'I thought you'd be pleased.'

'So did I, Charlie. Now, I'm not so sure.'

'Why?'

'Because...' said Munro, heaving a sigh. 'Because everything points to Hannah Lawson, everything we know suggests beyond doubt that she killed Harry, and Jason Chan, too. Now, this... this DNA on the overalls implicates Delgado, it places him at the scene, so how on earth he did he get that involved, Charlie? What's he not telling us?'

CHAPTER 18

"WHERE IS SHE NOW?"

'Ah, now that's a good question,' said Delgado. 'And I wish I knew, really I do, but like I told the Inspector, as far as I know, she's staying with friends, I think. A little break, a holiday of sorts. A job like hers can be quite taxing on the old grey matter. Most people only associate fatigue with manual labour, you know, physical work. They don't realise just how exhausting it can be using one's brain, day in, day out, planning, problem solving, working on strategies and all without spreadsheets. Still, all part of the package, I guess, if you're afflicted, like her. With the OCD, I mean. Everything has to be just right. Everything has to be perfect. There can be no trail.'

'Do you miss her?'

'I'm not sure. Yes, I think so. Not the company so much, more the... the thrill of the unexpected; I mean, you never knew what she was going to do next, what revelation would spill from her lips, not to mention where my next scar would be. I miss that. Life is, well, not dull, just a little less exciting, without her.'

'Did you regard her as your muse?'

'Very good, you make me sound like an artist of merit, sapping the energy of youth to feed my creative bent, but no, I wouldn't flatter myself that much. Not to say she wasn't inspirational, God, she opened up whole new avenues for me – subject matter, style – you know I even relinquished the oils for a spell, tried something new. Wasn't that successful, I have to admit, I mean, there's only so much one can tap from one's own veins before keeling over, you tend to get a bit dizzy, must be something to do with a lack of oxygen to the brain. I managed a couple of postcard-size studies but that...'

Delgado paused as the door opened.

'Interview suspended,' said Dr. Banham. '7.32am. Detective Inspector Munro and D.S. West have entered the room.'

'Jackie,' said Munro. 'Mind if we...'

'Of course not, James, do you want me to...'

'No, no,' said Munro. 'This won't take long, just a couple of...'

'So nice to see you again, Sergeant West,' said Delgado. 'Might I say, you look...'

'Mr Delgado,' said Munro tersely, as he tossed Lawson's ID card on the table. 'Is this the wee lassie you've been house-sitting for?'

Delgado smiled as he studied the card.

'Yes, yes that's her. Pretty isn't she? Oh, Hannah? So, that's her name – nice. It suits her, don't you think? Hannah.'

'Where is she?'

'I told you, I don't...'

Munro pulled back a chair and sat down. His voice was menacingly low, as though he were sealing a covert deal over a pint in a pub.

'Listen, Marcos,' he said, slowly pulling the house keys from his coat pocket. 'Listen carefully, because I'm not one for repeating myself.'

'I'm all ears, Inspector.'

'See these keys, here? Any idea what they'd be doing in Harry's apartment?'

'Harry's apartment?' said Delgado. 'Well, no...'

'Because we have evidence,' said Munro, 'photographic evidence, which shows them on his bed, shortly before he was murdered.'

'Murdered?' said Delgado, taken aback. 'Harry's been murdered? Outrageous! No, can't be true, you're trying to trick me; how could he possibly...'

'So, you see, this puts you in a very comprising situation. I'd start to worry if I were you.'

'But I told you,' said Delgado, his eyes darting from West to Banham and back again. 'They're not my keys, they're hers.'

'But your house keys are on the same chain.'

'Of course they are, makes it easier to carry them around.'

Munro sat back, folded his arms and stared at Delgado; his gaze unfaltering.

'Herongate Road,' he said.

'I'm sorry?'

'What were you doing in Herongate Road?'

'I...'

'You have a garden,' said Munro.

'Yes.'

'But it's not laid to lawn.'

'No.'

'So, why would you want a lawnmower?'

Delgado shifted uneasily in his seat.

'I don't know what you...'

'Are you a religious man, Marcos?' said Munro.

'Pardon? No, not really, why?'

'Oh, no reason, just think a wee prayer wouldnae go amiss. See, we found Jason Chan's DNA on your overalls.'

Delgado sniggered and shook his head.

'You're very good, Inspector,' he said, grinning. 'But you're barking up the wrong tree. There's absolutely no way those overalls could be mine, they wouldn't fit. They're too small. Way too small. They belong to…'

'Then why were they in your rucksack? At your house?'

'I… I carried them for her, she didn't have room in her…'

'So, you don't deny you were there, then?' said Munro. 'Herongate Road?'

Delgado sat back and glanced sheepishly at West.

'Well, okay, yes, hands up,' he said. 'I was there, but I didn't…'

'Didn't what?' said Munro.

'Kill him.'

'Who said he was dead?'

'Ah…'

'That makes you an accessory, Marcos. Problem is, I'm still not convinced. See, until our investigation takes a turn to the contrary, all the evidence suggests you murdered Jason Chan.'

'Preposterous!' said Delgado. 'How many times… I didn't…'

'Then who did?' said Munro. 'Who did?'

'It was… no. Nice try, Inspector. But I've never been one to speak ill of the dead. Look, as I've been telling your friend, the doctor, here, I don't know why I got involved. I made a mistake. I didn't kill him. I got carried away on a… on a tide of infatuation, I was caught up in the moment, but I knew it was wrong; underneath it all, I knew it was wrong. It made me feel sick.'

'Sick?' said Munro. 'It made you feel sick, but you didnae think to put a stop to it? To call the police and have her arrested? You thought it better to watch another man die?'

'No, no, of course not,' said Delgado.

Munro stood, placed his hands on the back of the chair and slid it carefully beneath the table.

'Final question,' he said. 'Where is she, Marcos? Where's Hannah?'

'Hannah? Oh, I'm getting bored, Inspector, she's gone to stay with…'

'I'll not ask again. Last chance.'

Delgado sat back, stretched his arms, and smiled.

'Alright, alright. I give up,' he said. 'She's at home.'

'At home?' said Munro.

'Yes, she never left. Oh, come on, you've searched her house, haven't you?'

'Aye, we have, indeed.'

'Then I'd go back and look again, Inspector. Look a little harder.'

* * *

The house was still. Munro, snapping on a pair of gloves, went to the lounge and opened the blinds. He lifted his head and took a deep breath. The scent of bleach had all but disappeared. West followed him upstairs, saying nothing, watching as he went from room to room, scouring the furnishings and floor coverings for signs of tampering, searching for that elusive hidey hole large enough to conceal a small body. He reached the bathroom and huffed.

'There's nowhere,' he said, confounded. 'There just doesn't seem to be…'

'What about the bath?' said West. 'Behind the bath panel, like Harry?'

'No,' said Munro. 'It's just not… something doesn't…'

'Patio? Under the paving slabs?'

'Too much like hard work. And that neighbour, she'd be…'

'Floorboards?' said West. 'Under the…'

'Wall to wall carpet. Charlie, look, everything's been cleared out, right?' said Munro, frustrated. 'The personal things, toiletries, jewellery, things you'd take with you if you were vacating the premises or going on your holidays. What else would you do? If you were going away, Charlie, what else…?'

'Put the rubbish out,' said West.

'Aye, he's done that.'

'Lock the doors and windows, make sure the cooker's off.'

Munro regarded her with a look of disdain.

'Oh, empty the fridge, make sure there's nothing going off, like milk or...'

'Charlie, there are none so blind,' said Munro, sparked with enthusiasm. 'Come on, I hope to God you're wrong, and please don't heave the contents of your stomach across the floor if we find something untoward.'

West stood by the sink nibbling her fingernails as Munro grasped the handle on the fridge door. He glanced at her briefly before tentatively easing it open. His head dropped.

'Charlie,' he said quietly, his face bathed in a soft, yellow light. 'Call Tommy. The usual please, pathologist, SOCOs, and we'll need a uniform on the door.'

'Right away. Can I…'

Munro took a pace back, allowing West an uninterrupted view of the contents. She peered inside. Hannah Lawson, eyes wide, wearing a bizarre, twisted grin on her decapitated head, stared back.

'It's odd,' she whispered. 'It's not as shocking, second time round.'

'You get used to it, in a way.'

'Where's the rest of her?'

Munro stepped forward and opened the lower door to the freezer, the shelves packed with an assortment of limbs, each neatly portioned up and sealed in freezer bags.

'How long do you think she's been here?' said West, finding it impossible not to gawp.

'Hard to say,' said Munro. 'But it's a three-star appliance, she'll not go off in a hurry.'

West smiled.

'I don't know why I find that funny,' she said.

'Humour. It's the only way I can deal with it,' said Munro, placing a hand on her shoulder. 'Now, away lassie. I think you've seen enough.'

They stood side by side on the doorstep, under the watchful eye of the overly-inquisitive neighbour until, four minutes later, Sergeant Cole careered around the corner accompanied by two constables.

'Guv,' said Cole. 'Miss. You alright? You look like you've seen a...'

'It's Hannah Lawson, Sergeant. Or Annabel Parkes. She's in the... in the fridge.'

'What?'

'And the freezer,' said West. 'Tell them, when they get here, no hanging around; DNA, dentals, anything they can find. We need to know who she is, as soon as possible.'

'Might be tough, miss,' said Cole. 'Seeing as how she doesn't seem to exist.'

* * *

The bench, concluded Dr. Banham as she waited patiently for Munro to return, was about as comfortable as a church pew. Dictaphone in hand, she listened back over her interview while the duty officer on the front desk flicked apathetically through a copy of *The Racing Post*.

'Jackie,' said Munro as he greeted her warmly. 'You didnae have to wait. Will we go upstairs?'

'Thanks, no, I'm a bit pushed for time now.'

'Okay, so, how was it? What do you think?'

'Well, interesting, to say the least,' said Banham. 'I think he'll make a good case study once the trial's out of the way. Students could learn a lot from this one.'

'Is that so?' said Munro. 'And that would be why? A split personality? Psychotic tendencies, perhaps?'

'I'm afraid not, James. Look, I don't know where you are with your investigation but if you do find him guilty, I really can't see his defence claiming diminished responsibility, or coercion, even.'

159

'Really?' said Munro. 'Why not?'

'No grounds,' said Banham. 'As far as I'm concerned, he's as sane as sixpence, James. Sane as sixpence.'

* * *

West sat motionless as Delgado, head on hands, gazed at her across the table in the interview room.

'You know,' he said. 'You really are quite attractive. Maybe we could...'

She stabbed the red button on the interview recorder as the door opened and a uniformed constable entered the room, followed by a stern-looking Munro.

'Marcos Delgado,' he said, standing, hands clasped behind his back. 'I am arresting you for the murders of Jason Chan and...'

'What?' said Delgado, rising to his feet. 'You can't be serious, I've already told you, I had nothing...'

'...and Hannah Lawson. You do not have to say anything but it may harm your defence if you do not mention, when questioned, something you later rely on in court. Anything you do say, may be given in evidence. Do you understand?'

'I told you,' said Delgado, as the constable cuffed his hands behind his back and led him away. 'I had nothing to do with Jason Chan...'

'Do you understand?'

'Yes, but...'

* * *

Munro, leaning against the window frame, stared pensively out across the green, oblivious to the unnecessarily loud tinkling of a spoon in a teacup as West summoned up a brew.

'Penny for them?' she said softly, handing him a cup.

Munro smiled, warmed by the unexpected gesture.

'Oh, nothing important,' he said. 'This and that, anything and everything. Lawson, Delgado. Home.'

160

'Home? You mean home, home? Scotland?'

'Aye. I think it's time. You know, I'm not one to say this often, Charlie,' said Munro, raising his mug. 'But I could murder a drink, and I don't mean this.'

'Ooh, you're not kidding,' said West. 'Large vodka and tonic – tastes better when you've earned it. Tell you what, it's on me. Come on.'

'Come on?' said Munro. 'Charlie, are you not keen on tying up the loose ends?'

'Loose ends?'

'For a start, we still cannae say, conclusively, who killed Jason Chan.'

'But Delgado's admitted he was there,' said West. 'Just a matter of time before he tells us what we already know. And anyway, he's virtually confessed to murdering Lawson, so we've got him, haven't we?'

'We have but, but why? He was head over heels in love with her, why kill her?'

'He told us why,' said West. 'He got carried away, love makes you do stupid things.'

'Maybe,' said Munro. 'But we still don't know who she is, do we? I'm telling you, if we cannae get a match off her DNA, we're scuppered. I don't like loose ends, Charlie. They're like bootlaces. They can trip you up.'

West stared into her teacup and sighed.

'So, we've still got some work to do, eh? Probably too early for a drink, anyway.'

* * *

Delgado, locked in a holding cell, had made himself at home, lying, as he was, flat on his back with his legs crossed and his arms folded behind his head.

'Hello,' he said cheerfully, sitting up as Munro and West arrived. 'How's tricks?'

Munro turned to West, frowned, and focused his attention on Delgado.

'Do you have a screw loose?' he said incredulously.

161

'I beg your pardon?'

'You, you've just been charged on two counts of murder and you're lying there like you're on a mini break in Torremolinos.'

'I know,' said Delgado, grinning. 'Bonkers, isn't it? But what else can I do? I've made my bed, and now...'

Munro looked at West who was doing her utmost to suppress a smile.

'I'm having doubts about Jackie Banham,' he mumbled. 'Are you sure you're not on medication?'

'Quite sure,' said Delgado.

'And you're still refusing a lawyer? Do you realise what that means?'

'I do. Look, I'm guilty, I'm not going to plead otherwise, a lawyer would be a horrendous waste of taxpayers' money, in fact, you could save a small fortune by doing away with the hearing too and just locking me up. A spell inside sounds quite inviting, no distractions, food and board, plenty of time to concentrate on my paintings. Got a lot of stuff I want to put down.'

'Good grief,' said Munro, confounded by Delgado's disposition. 'You know, I can honestly say, in all my years on the force, I have never, never, met anyone like you.'

'That's a very nice compliment, thank you,' said Delgado.

'Are you comfortable, Marcos?' said West, allowing the smile to creep across her face. 'Do you need anything?'

'Very kind, but no. I'm fine, thanks.'

'I hate to say this,' said Munro, with a sigh, 'but I can't help but think you're a fundamentally decent chap. It's a shame you'll not see daylight for the foreseeable.'

'You're embarrassing me, now, Inspector; in front of the lovely Sergeant, too.'

'One last thing.'

'Name it.'

'I need you to satisfy my curiosity here,' said Munro. 'I need to know why. You loved her, you were infatuated with her. Why did you kill her?'

Delgado hesitated as he searched for the right words, his hands clasped together beneath his chin as though he were praying.

'It was a heat of the moment thing,' he said. 'No malice aforethought, no cunning plan, not even a hint of retribution. It was totally impulsive, but not in a bad way. It's what she wanted. I know now, of course, it could have been avoided, if I'd been stronger, if I'd put my foot down, but I guess we just got, I got, carried away.'

'Go on.'

'She liked pain. She got a kick out of it. She liked me to use the scalpel on her, where it wouldn't show. We were getting, shall we say, intimate, and she cut me, along my back. The blade was that sharp, I barely felt it. Then she begged me to do the same to her so, willingly, I obliged. Then, she turned over and pointed to her neck. I refused. I said it was too dangerous but she insisted, she wrapped her legs around my back and wouldn't let go. Eventually, I caved in. I made a couple of small cuts, token cuts, very superficial, low down, so she could hide them, but it wasn't enough. She kept egging me on, "deeper" she said. Then she grabbed my hand and drew the blade across her neck. Before I knew what was happening, there was blood everywhere, down my hands, all over the pillow and the sheets, and yet, all the time, she was groaning, if you don't mind me saying so, Sergeant, with pleasure. Smiling and groaning. Then... then she just, slipped away. Sounds bizarre, but it was very peaceful. Like she'd drifted off to sleep.'

CHAPTER 19

SPRATT HALL ROAD, WANSTEAD. 11:28am
Save for the rhythmic ticking of the wall clock, not a
sound could be heard. Munro, indulging himself with his
favourite past-time, contemplated the green below whilst
West, cradling her coffee, perused the benefits of a detox
weekend on the Holy Isle. Her cup, unfortunately, left her
hands rather abruptly as Sergeant Cole barged through the
door, shattering the peace and causing Munro to spin in
his chair.

'Guv, miss,' he said excitedly, waving a large envelope.
'Hot off the press, from the lab. The stuff on Lawson, I
mean Annabel.'

'I'll take it,' said West, pointing to the floor. 'If you
wouldn't mind, Sergeant. There's a cloth on the side.'

Munro leaned back in his chair and waited patiently as
West read through the pages, raising her eyebrows as she
hit the salient points. Her jaw dropped as she reached the
last page and turned to face Munro.

'Catching flies?' he said. 'Slowly, now, Charlie. One
point at a time. Let's have it.'

West took a deep breath as Sergeant Cole looked on.

'You were right,' she said. 'The DNA on the scalpel, the one we took from Delgado's place, it matches Hannah Lawson.'

'Good,' said Munro. 'Positive proof, which supports his confession. Guilty as charged. That only leaves one loose end. How about it, Charlie? Are they going to send me home a happy man?'

West flicked back to the final page in the envelope.

'Well, yes and no,' she said. 'They have actually found a match to her DNA on the system, bad news is, it's no-one called Hannah Lawson...'

'Dear, dear.'

'Or Annabel Parkes.'

'Well?'

'It's Aileen...'

'Aileen?' said Munro, leaping to his feet. 'Why, that's the lassie the real Annabel Parkes mentioned, the one peddling dope at the university.'

'Yup, and I'm surprised you've not heard of her, she's from your neck of the woods.'

'Of course,' said Munro. 'How silly of me, after all, there's only two Aileens in the whole of Scotland and one of those is in Inverness.'

'Really? Sorry,' said West, 'being silly, aren't I? Anyway, she went to school in Stranraer, left when her father died and did an apprenticeship with a butcher on Hanover Street before moving south. You'll like this, apparently her father was shot dead in his car. Never found the...'

'I need a name, Charlie!' yelled Munro. 'For heaven's sake, I need a name.'

'Alright, alright, it's... MacAdam. Aileen MacAdam.'

Munro slumped back in his chair and blew a hefty sigh.

'Well, well, well,' he said quietly. 'They were right along. The past does come back to haunt you. Never even knew he had a daughter.'

'What?' said West. 'Who? I don't get it, what are you...shit! That's him, isn't it? Her dad, he's the one who torched your house, he killed your...'

'He did that, Charlie. He did that.'

'Bloody hell, hold on, that picture of you, the old paper clipping in the wardrobe, she didn't have that because she knew you were on to her, she had it because you were next on the list. You were the "special thing" she was...'

'Aye, I'd say so,' said Munro. 'Och, and I do so hate to disappoint.'

CHAPTER 20

OSPRINGE HOUSE, WOOTTON STREET, SE1. 9:17am

If one regarded funerals as morbid affairs attended by distant relatives stricken with grief, coupled with copious amounts of wailing and saddled with tears, as opposed to a joyous celebration of the dearly departed, then the weather could not have been more appropriate. Thick, low cloud – as dark as Hades and rumbling with the threat of an imminent deluge – rolled overhead. Samantha Baker, still in two minds about attending, regarded such an occasion as neither. To her, seeing a casket lowered into a mechanically dug hole and subsequently covered with sodden earth, was nothing more than a precursor to the inevitable gathering at the family home, which meant free food, free drinks and, no doubt, an assortment of single men wearing sharp, well-tailored suits.

She finished her coffee, stubbed out her cigarette and turned her attention to the mirror. Black, as well as being regarded as the most suitable form of attire when bidding farewell to those who had given up the mortal coil, was also, coincidentally, the mainstay of her wardrobe. There was nothing in the rule book that said one couldn't look fashionable as well as suitably morose. She gazed at her reflection and pursed her lips as she awarded herself a narcissistic seal of approval. She was, she told herself, smoking hot. The black turtle-neck sweater set off her bottle-blonde bob, the black skinny jeans accentuated her lithe legs and the black leather bomber added a degree of youthful, street-cred. The only item of clothing that might have been deemed somewhat incongruous, particularly amongst the older generation, was her choice footwear. White, and perhaps, a tad too casual. She didn't care, her Converse boots were the most comfortable things she'd ever worn, moreover, they were achingly cool.

She checked her watch as the rain began to rattle the windows and decided the trip would be worth the effort. She opened the door and shuddered, dropping her keys as a crack of thunder exploded almost overhead. Waterloo station was but a hop and a skip away, her trusty hat would save her from a drenching.

She smiled as she bent to pick them up, cursing herself for feeling momentarily sentimental. It was a gift from Harry, the key fob. He'd given it to her on his return from Skyros. Not much, so far as gifts go, but it was better than the predictable bottle of Metaxa, Ouzo or virgin olive oil. It was 'special'. 'Hardly anyone has them here,' he'd said. 'unless you're Greek or Turkish, so it's quite unique, almost original, in a way. It's called a Mati.'

If you enjoyed this book, please let others know by leaving a quick review on Amazon. Also, if you spot anything untoward in the paperback, get in touch. We strive for the best quality and appreciate reader feedback.

editor@thebookfolks.com

www.thebookfolks.com